A COMEDY OF TERRORS

Thanks, Moira, hope you enjoy this.
John M. Robertson

2475-ALLE

A COMEDY OF TERRORS

John M. Robertson

2475-ALLE

ISBN #: Softcover 0-7388-3293-6

This is a work of fiction. Names, characters, places and incidents either are the product of the author's imagination or are used fictitiously, and any resemblance to any actual persons, living or dead, events, or locales is entirely coincidental.

This book was printed in the United States of America.

To order additional copies of this book, contact:
Xlibris Corporation
1-888-7-XLIBRIS
www.Xlibris.com
Orders@Xlibris.com

CONTENTS

CHAPTER 1

The cocktail party seemed to be a success, but Lawton was not enjoying it. The problem was that everyone else was dressed, while he was doing his mingling mother naked. President Reagan was there, the Chairman of the Board was there with her secretary, and a great many people he had never met before made a point of introducing themselves. And yet no one seemed to have noticed. But he knew it was going to get worse. It always did. Apart from the embarrassment, he knew there was some horror hovering just beyond his consciousness, waiting to pounce. And then, just before the suspense became too much to bear, with infinite gratefulness he became aware that it could only be a dream, and all he had to do was go to sleep again and by morning the horror and the embarrassment would all be gone.

Lawton Wainright sat at his desk and recalled every detail. Why did he keep having these nakedness dreams?

They must have begun some time after the earthquake, when he had been in his bath and his only thought had been, "I can't run outside with no clothes on." His greatest fear had always been of embarrassing himself in public.

At the clamor of the distant bell, Lawton pushed black rimmed glasses higher on a freckled nose, slipped back half an inch of white shirtcuff on his right wrist and checked the time by his Rolex. Thirty-five seconds past five o'clock. His Rolex was never wrong, so the time switch on the bell circuit must need adjusting. The pen tray was already parallel with the edge of the desk, but after some thought he placed it carefully in the desk drawer. There was always the risk of a cleaning person accidentally displacing it, or worse, knocking it to the floor. Lawton Wainright would deny that he was a fussy man, but since everything had its place, he felt that in his life at least everything should be in its proper place. And the place of a pen tray was not on the floor, particularly the pen tray of the Curator of the Museum of Anthropology. Though it should not be supposed that Doctor Wainright felt himself superior to other mortals; it was just that he had a well tuned sense of the fitness of things, and it seemed only fitting that the incumbent of such a responsible position, and his property, should be afforded due respect.

The numbed silence that followed the bell was abruptly shattered by an irreverent double rap at the communicating door leading from his secretary's office. A cascade of corn colored hair, two wide round blue eyes and an eager smile appeared suddenly round the edge of the door.

"We've thrown out the last of the customers, Doctor Wainright," announced the eager smile breathlessly. "Mister Topham has locked the doors and now he's looking for bombs and things."

Lawton Wainright may not actually have flinched, but he blenched inwardly.

"Miss Saunders, a museum does not have customers. We prefer to call them visitors. And for the peace of mind of all of us it would be better if you referred to the Commissionaire's duties as the Evening Security Check." He bestowed an encouraging smile, one that would indicate this was not a formal reprimand so much as a gentle correction of a new and inexperienced employee. It was essential to maintain the dignity of the establishment, yet at the same time keep staff relations friendly enough though not familiar. Miss Saunders was certainly a most attractive young woman. About twenty-seven at a guess.

As he smiled at her, he permitted himself a brief comparison with the young woman who would be there when he arrived home. About the same age, he thought. But if only Claire were as vivacious! And eager! Claire was certainly attractive enough to look at, with her wicked green eyes and cascading red hair. She had been lively and pretty when they first married, but now her mouth too often had a downward pout and the eagerness seemed to have drained away as she discovered that life with a scientist was not to be the round of social soirees she had been brought up to expect.

Miss Saunders smiled back and permitted herself to wonder, for the seventh time that day, what a good-looking, dark haired, six foot, thirty two years old museum curator would be like in bed. And what the effect would be if she were to ask him.

Instead she asked, "Will you be staying late tonight, Doctor Wainright?"

"No, Miss Saunders," he said. "I don't want to be home late. Mrs. Wainright and I are making a little safari into foreign territory this evening. We are going with some friends to the Tight Owl night club."

Good god, thought Miss Saunders, who'd have thought it? Like to get him tight as an owl and see what develops.

But she had learned in her twenty-six years not to express such thoughts. She merely observed with some enthusiasm, "The Tight Owl's a great spot. Have you been there before?"

She came from behind the door into the room, revealing a tightly fitting pale blue sweater, nipples that protruded sufficiently to be obtrusive, and an extraordinarily slim waist held in check by a heavy gold slave chain. In that order. That, at any rate, was the order in which Lawton Wainright noticed, and noted, the details. Though not for the first time.

"No," he said, "this will be a new experience."

"Charlie Chesney's opening there tonight," she said, well aware that her boss's eyes had left hers and were focused elsewhere. "He's fantastic. Wouldn't it be fun to meet him?"

Lawton Wainright's self discipline and sense of decorum would not allow his mind to dwell on any ideas that Miss Saunders' mention of fun might conjure up. "It promises to be a very pleasant evening," he allowed, and left it at that.

On the drive home Miss Saunders, with no such problems of self-discipline, allowed her mind to dwell at great length on a great many such ideas. This was her first day as Doctor

Wainright's secretary. Her boss was nice mannered, well dressed, educated, dark hair rather long like a poet or a conductor, beautiful deepset brown eyes and the dreamiest Errol Flynn mustache. And stuffy. And sexy as hell if you were attracted by the subtle hint of sadness and vulnerability. Which she certainly was. She wondered about his home life. And his sex life. And then allowed her musings to roam further.

It is doubtful if Lawton Wainright would have approved. He would certainly have been embarrassed.

Later that evening, the safari into foreign territory proved, at first, to be more successful than anyone expected. Lawton still tried his hardest to please Claire, in little daily ways and in planning events that would give pleasure to her. He had been brought up to believe that you got out of marriage only what you put into it, and though Claire's attitude was more and more that she had already given at the office, it was not in his nature to reduce his contribution. When Jeff had suggested the Tight Owl, half facetiously, his first thought had been that it would only cause Claire to get into an upset about clothes. He had never been sure whether she was easily upset, really upset, or whether she simply used the occasion to demand attention. However, Margie had decided it was a good idea, for her and Jeff, for Lawton, and even for Claire. And when Margie made up her mind there was no need for further discussion.

"Leave it to me. I'll call her tomorrow," Margie had said. "No-one worries about clothes these days, and I'll say it's for Jeff's birthday next week. She'll have to come."

Jeff had been more concerned with getting Lawton out for a night on the town. They had been out for a few beers occasionally since University days, but Claire resented being left at home alone and yet refused to join them, and the meetings were becoming less frequent.

"Lawton deserves a night out," he had said to Margie before they left for the club. "It's not much of a life with her. But I don't suppose the silly cow will enjoy it. I'll lay you six to four Charlie Chesney doesn't get a single laugh out of her."

But Margie always saw the best in everyone. "She's not that bad, honey. She really came out of herself at the Christmas party."

"Only because everyone made her the center of everything," Jeff said. "It burns me up the way he worships her, and the snarky bitch does nothing but complain."

So, though all three of them set out that evening less with expectations of enjoyment than with a sense of mission, they were pleasantly surprised. The evening went well.

Until the last. Plying Claire with Hawaiian boomerangs was Margie's idea, and it worked well. The food was excellent, and Claire's cracked crab kept her too busy to complain. Jeff had made certain financial arrangements with the waiter, who paid such special attention to Claire that her perpetual pout finally turned up at the corners. Even Cheerful Charlie Chesney seemed to be part of the conspiracy, sitting at the piano and dedicating a new song to 'the lady with the glorious red hair.'

But, inevitably, it was Claire who decided it was time to go, and insisted on leaving five minutes into the monologue.

It was at that moment that the countdown to a nightmare seems to have begun.

It was ten fifteen in the evening.

CHAPTER 2

Charles Delano Chesney always liked to tell people he was born backstage in a costume trunk. In fact, his start in show business had been with a different kind of trunk. He was fifteen years old when the Marston Brothers' Circus visited town. When the circus left six days later, Charlie left with it, working for the man who cleaned the elephants. Apprenticed to a manure shoveller, he liked to say. Within four years, he had decided that elephants and clowns and ladies in tights and hauling on guy ropes and moving on every few days were losing their glamor. He had out-comicked the comedians, and given a new dimension to the clowns' act. He had served his time with the band. He had learned to ride bareback. He had even tried out on the high wire. Once.

So he left the circus behind. And at the age of thirty seven, brash and confident, he was on his way to the top. He had an act that was different because it could not be defined, because it combined so many talents that had been both inherited and learned, and because he liked to include his audience in the act. An Evening With Cheerful Charlie Chesney meant music and humor and comedy (he maintained the two were entirely different) and variety and burlesque and Shakespeare and satire. At the very least.

The opening at the Tight Owl was one more success on the ladder. When the monologue ended, there was a standing ovation. It had been a great act. After the applause he retired to his dressing room. It was less a retirement, really, than a parade. First his agent took him by the arm, three twittering nymphs following in line astern like a flotilla of baby ducks. "Great act, Charlie, best yet. I've got three little admirers here who want your autograph. Sign these photos for them, will ya?"

"Sure, Marvin, any time." Chesney took the pictures from the agent's hands and flashed a photogenic smile.

"Glad you enjoyed the show," he said collectively, and wrote on each of the pictures, 'Love you baby, Charlie Chesney.'

"Swell of you to come tonight, Marvin," he said to the agent, and moved toward the dressing room.

"Couldn't keep me away from an opening, Charlie. Ever know me to miss one?"

Chesney turned to the three ducklings still following behind. "Just like brothers we are. Inseparable. Joined at the heart by a common percentage. Hi, Linda baby. Marvin, you haven't met my fiancée, Linda McClusky."

The lady referred to showed no surprise at this euphemism, though certainly marriage had at no time been on the menu during the five hectic evenings and impassioned nights since she had inherited Chesney from a taxi driver with a sharp business sense.

"He's passed out, and there's ten and a quarter on the meter," the taxi driver had said. "Pay the fare and you can have him with the cab. It's Cheerful Charlie Chesney, so maybe you can take him back for a refund in the morning."

But she had not taken him back. She found him penitent, apologetic and amusing. He was good looking, though his eyes and his cheeks certainly were a little puffy from too much drinking. His dark hair was always tousled in a boyish way, and his mouth was just enough lop-sided to give him a permanent impish grin. He was a celebrity, sexy, and apparently without any major flaw apart from his drinking, so ten and a quarter cab fare and breakfast seemed a small enough investment for the opportunity to know him at close quarters.

She had followed his social adventures through the tabloids for long enough to know that a great many young ladies had invested a great deal more in the attempt to ensnare him. Though ensnarement never entered her head. After five days, she was well enough aware that Charlie Chesney was not about to become a married man come hell, high water or lawsuit.

As the six of them progressed toward the dressing room, the parade was swollen by the addition of two writers, the club manager. a producer, a young man named Harvey and several young ladies also addressed as 'Baby' who appeared to be discards from previous games.

"Gin and tonic, tall one, somebody. Linda Baby, you know where it is, be a love. I need a whole jugful, it's hot out there. Don't know how the customers stand it."

Chesney threw off his dinner jacket and tie, and sprawled into a chair. "How'd it go? Seemed all right to me. Needs a little tightening in places. Sorry if I loused up your sound, Harvey, but I couldn't of sat on that piano stool another minute. My pants were sticking to my ass like I was sitting in honey, know what I mean? Had to get up and cool things off. Larry, that rabbit joke didn't go worth a damn, we'll have to do something with it. But they really got the mermaid and the polar bear didn't they just? Was that one of yours, Merv? I had an idea out there, can't we do something about this guy who's Reagan's joke writer having to hire a translator ready for the next summit with Gorbachov? See what you can make of it. Say, did you see those horses' asses get up and walk out right in the middle of the monologue? After I dedicated Springtime in the Bronx to that red haired broad? Funny thing, the guy with the glasses held out his hands like he was apologizing. Nice guy. I kinda felt sorry for him."

At eleven twenty seven, some one hour and three jugs of gin and tonic later, the post mortem and the congratulations were over, and Linda and Charlie arrived back at the Chesney apartment. Linda was fast learning what was involved in playing the part of consort to a celebrity, and she was not at all sure she could keep pace with him. Presumably what he wanted was a girl with his kind of stamina, one who could party with him whenever he was in the mood. But Linda was not a party girl, or never had been until then. And she looked nothing like the compliant young starlets who seemed to be constantly swept into Charlie's orbit. More like a country schoolmarm, Charlie had told her, owl-like glasses and a fresh-scrubbed cleanness, brown curly hair close to the head and a certain shyness among the hearty back-stage crowd.

However, without her glasses and without her clothes, there was nothing of the country girl, or the shyness. She delighted in striking a pose to watch the effect it had on Charlie.

"Linda baby, I've never seen tits that sit up and beg like that," he said in admiration their second night together, when he was in a better condition to appreciate them than he had been the first night. "And those legs, I swear they go all the way up to your armpits. Put your glasses on, Hon, and make like I'm laying a farmer's daughter."

What Charlie really needed, Linda decided, was a girl who could convince him that marathon partying could be injurious to health. She had bought him, it seemed, for ten and a quarter, and now she felt responsible for him. There was the very real possibility that if she put on the brakes she would lose him sooner rather than later, and she was enjoying being with him. But that was a risk she would have to take. He's going to get hooked by some rotten little hooker sooner or later anyway, was the way she rationalized it to herself, so what the hell? He's a nice guy, and he deserves more than just someone to help him spend his money.

The alternative to life in the fast lane seemed to lie in the bedroom, but again Linda doubted that her stamina could match Charlie's. She was out of practice, she thought. Or, really, she'd never even been in this league. Screw middle class morals anyway, they leave a girl unprepared for situations like this.

By eleven fifty nine, her middle class morals were being shattered once again. They both found it a pleasant experience.

"Let's dance, Linda Baby," Charlie said, switching on the stereo in the bedroom.

"But Mister Chesney, I'm not accustomed to dancing in gentlemen's bedrooms," she replied demurely.

He held her close, pressing her body against his. "Whose bedrooms are you accustomed to dancing in, for Pete's sake?"

"That's not exactly what I meant," she said. "I meant I'm not accustomed to dancing in *gentlemen's bedrooms*."

"That's a helluvan admission." He moved his hands down her back to cup her rear. "Just what are you accustomed to doing in gentlemen's bedrooms?"

"Certainly not this. Do you realize your hands are in a very intimate place?"

"I should do. I put them there." As they moved to the music he put his right thigh between hers, pressing into her. "If you think that's intimate, just wait till I get warmed up."

"If you do that any more I'm not sure I shall be able to wait," she gasped. "And as for getting warmed up, it already feels pretty hot to me."

He grinned wolfishly. "Well now, that's the first time anyone's ever called it pretty. Hot, yes. But not pretty."

His fingers were sliding down the zipper of her dress, then slipping the dress forward over her shoulders. "We don't want anything to happen to this pretty dress, do we?"

"It's not what's going to happen to the dress that concerns me." She pushed away from him, and let the dress slip down over her hips to the floor. "It's what's going to happen to me."

He had more difficulty with the fastening of her brassiere. "If you're a good girl nothing will happen to you."

"That's a rotten thing to say to a girl when you've got her half naked. How would you like me to say that to you?"

"I don't see how you could. I'm not a girl. I wouldn't make a good girl anyway."

"You certainly would. You'd make any kind of girl you could get your hands on. I was a good girl until I met you. And take your jacket off, it's hurting my breasts."

"Tits," Charlie said. "Breasts when they're respectable, tits when they're naked. And these little beauties sure are naked." He let his arms drop to his side so that she could push off his jacket and undo his shirt. He put his mouth to hers while they danced.

At length, when she had her breath back, "If this is your idea of giving a girl a good time I'm going home."

"You'd be arrested," he said, holding her at arms length and admiring her. "For stopping the traffic. I thought you liked dancing."

"This isn't dancing, it's a strip-tease. And very one-sided at that."

He stepped back, and slapped his head with the flat of his hand, a gesture from his act. "Complaints. All I get is complaints. Forty million people are clamoring to see Cheerful Charlie Chesney, but you have to complain."

"Forty million people haven't been peeled to their bare necessities," she countered. "All I want is equal opportunity. No descrimination. You've got me in a condition to stop the traffic and what have I got to look at? A few hairs on your chest. A girl's at a disadvantage in a situation like this."

"But look at the other advantages you get," he said.

"How can I look at them if you're going to stay fully dressed like that. Anyway, I wouldn't exactly call them advantages. I could make a nice living undressed just as I am, but who's going to pay to see you stripped to the buff?"

"All you girls want is a man's body," he complained, dramatically unbuckling his belt and pulling down his zipper. "Is this what you want? I won't be responsible for the consequences. And just leave my buff out of this. Charlie Chesney's buff is not for sale. Or hire."

"Doesn't look as if it could get much higher." She giggled, and quickly stepped out of her panties.

"Don't you believe it, darling," he said quietly as she came to him. "Chesney's going to rise to new heights tonight."

* * *

At eleven twenty two, Mr. and Mrs. Lawton Wainright arrived home at 67, Croftdown Road. Eight years before, when they were first married, Claire had decided that the curator of an important museum should live in the prestigious University District. Lawton had been concerned about economy, so they had bought a modest size house, all on one level, well shaded by trees and not overlooked by neighbors. So they were well out in the suburbs, an hour from downtown.

The drive home from the Tight Owl had been a silent one, Claire tight-lipped and vengeful, Lawton miserable and blaming himself for even suggesting the evening out. As they parted from Jeff and Margie outside the club, he had taken Jeff aside and quietly apologized for cutting the evening short. He had tried not to make it seem like a deliberate dig at Claire, but she had taken offence instantly, and with Claire that meant he had to be punished.

He dreaded these occasions, particularly since he had no idea how to cope with them. They always began with the silent treatment, and ended with a noisy tirade. It was as if Claire consciously planned the technique for maximum effect. During the long silences, when she refused to answer him and occupied herself with combing her hair or carefully attending to her make-up while she hummed to herself, he had time to analyze the reason for the row, and always came to the realization that he might have avoided it if he had acted differently. By the time she was ready for the second phase, he was blaming himself, remorseful and wretched at his inability to handle the situation better, yet fully aware that he was being manipulated.

Then, as if she had followed his train of thought, she would play on his guilt. "I suppose you're proud of yourself for upsetting me like this," was her usual opening.

He had exhausted all the meaningful replies, which anyway only inflamed her. This time he said nothing, and went miserably to the bedroom to undress. But silence was equally inflammatory. She catalogued the occasions in the past when his thoughtlessness or deliberate unpleasantness had upset her, her voice rising and increasing in stridency.

"And if you think you're going to sleep beside me you can think again," she climaxed. "You can sleep in the guest room. God knows we never seem to have any guests."

This was another of her complaints, one that played equally strongly on his guilt. Lawton was well aware he was not a gregarious person. They had few close friends, and their social life was certainly not full or exciting. Not as full or exciting as Claire wanted. And as with all her other complaints, he felt himself ultimately to blame. But this time something seemed to snap in his usually rigid self-control. A rising wave of fury at being constantly trapped, constantly in the wrong, brought out the only sharp retort he had ever made to her during two years of increasingly bitter strife.

"Only a deaf mute could get any sleep beside you," he shouted through the open door, despising himself for raising his voice, and resenting her for making him do it. "And if you're so desperately fond of the guest room you can move in there yourself. You're not driving me out of my own bed."

He slammed the bedroom door shut, looked about for something to hold it closed against the expected onslaught, and tilted his valet chair under the doorknob. "Damn you, damn you, damn you!" he exploded, his eyes filling with tears. "I can forgive you most things, but not for making me behave like this. I suppose that's what you really want, to break me down."

He hung his suit in the tall, wall-length closet with the sliding doors, ruefully aware of the way Claire's clothes were forcing his to one end. His shirt and underclothes he hung neatly over one of Claire's chairs. His pajamas were under the pillow of the left-hand bed. The double bed had been exchanged eighteen months before, at Claire's insistence, for two separate beds.

The tall valet chair, with its coat hanger back and receptacles for keys and money, was the only masculine feature of the room. Everything else, the gold satin headboards on the beds, the cluttered dressing table, the thick pastel colored rugs, the pale blue scalloped drapes, the framed cut-outs from fashion magazines on the wall, made the room a feminine domain.

"At least I have my own bed," he thought, as he pulled back the cover.

At eleven fifty nine, just at the moment when Linda McClusky and Charlie Chesney were beginning their countdown to bed, Lawton Wainright climbed into his bed. He took off his glasses and put them carefully on the bedside table, switched off the light, and resigned himself to another sleepless night as his mind replayed every detail of yet another row. But within a minute he was asleep, to lie undisturbed until nine twenty three the next morning.

The next morning was to be the first day of a new life for Lawton Wainright.

CHAPTER 3

Lawton Wainright woke suddenly out of a deep sleep, inexplicably, perhaps disturbed by a sound from outside. There was a sour taste in his mouth, a foulness and dryness, and his head throbbed. With his eyes still closed, he considered. Tastes like the aftermath of too much alcohol, he thought. But I hardly drank anything last night. I haven't done anything to deserve a hangover since Jeff and I tied one on at alumni night two, three years ago. With some effort he opened his eyes. The lids of one were sticking together, and it was some moments before he could get them unglued. The light from the window immediately beside him dazzled. He shut it out again quickly, though not so much because of the brightness as to put a stop to the vertigo that flowed over him as the window with its bright orange drapes kept sailing past.

Like a record with a crack in it, he thought, unconsciously focusing on analyzing the phenomenon to take his mind off the nausea. Only in video. The after image of the golden light past the orange drapes still burned into his retina.

Orange drapes? WE DON'T HAVE ORANGE DRAPES! There were no orange drapes in the house. Anywhere. Claire would never have approved. He opened his eyes to face the glare from the window again. Between the drapes, he could see that the window was in fact a pair of sliding glass doors opening onto a balcony outside, with a view of tall buildings beyond. The glass doors and the balcony and the orange drapes continued sailing by, but that had lost its importance. What mattered was that he knew there were no glass doors anywhere in the house. Or a balcony. There wasn't even a window of any sort beside the bed. This couldn't be his bedroom. OR EVEN HIS HOUSE!

He sat up in bed frantically, ignoring the drumming head and the nausea. It was The Dream again, he knew, the recurring dream, mother naked and people coming and going and he was the only one without clothes. He felt beneath the bedclothes, praying to find pajamas. But as always in the dream he was naked. The horror began to build up, but as he always did, he talked sharply to himself. Go back to sleep and everything will be all right in the morning.

Thankfully he lay down again and closed his eyes. But there was no sleep. The bed was solid and real. And when he opened his eyes, the same ceiling and walls were there, real, and foreign. He had never seen them before, even in his dream. And still he was undressed. He reached for his glasses on the table beside the bed. They were missing. Panic began to well up inside him. For a few moments he lay whimpering, terrified and unthinking. He made an effort to fight it down at last, searching for a rational explanation. Perhaps he went home to Jeff's place last night? But the memory of the row before he went to bed was too clear. He could replay every word of it. He took comfort in recalling the details, a link with rationality. But they meant this wasn't a dream, it was really happening, and again he felt the panic rising.

He forced himself to think calmly, to analyze, to blot out the fear. Had he been kidnapped? Drugged? Was this sourness in his mouth what dope tasted like? Perhaps this was a hospital? Or a hotel? Of course, he walked out on Claire and came to a hotel, and got good and drunk. It wasn't like him, but it explained the strange room, and the taste in his mouth, and not being able to remember. And he wouldn't have taken his pajamas with him.

Relief surged over him. He had never slept without pajamas, never in his life, not even at camp. It seemed somehow lascivious, and he felt so vulnerable. What if the place caught fire and he had to run outside without any clothes? It was a Sunday, he remembered, so he could take his time about getting up, though it would be terrible to be surprised without pajamas by the maid coming to make up the room.

Then there was the unpleasantness with Claire to be considered, or was that just a dream? No, it must have happened or he wouldn't be in a hotel. Well, the longer that confrontation was delayed the better. She would be even harder to talk to when she discovered he had walked out.

He opened his eyes again and sat up carefully, ignoring the physical distress in his relief at being free of the panic. He considered the bedroom. It was large and bright, with the morning sun streaming in through the glass doors. At least, he assumed it must be the morning sun. He certainly hoped so. He had always considered orange drapes the height of bad taste, but they certainly brightened the room. Probably he was a snob. Jeff often said so. It was a double bed, king-size or queen-size, he could never tell the difference. They looked like watercolors on the wall, small and nicely framed. Gilt framed mirror. A rather nice tapestry-finish wing-back chair, and his clothes scattered on the floor beside it. Yet he was always most careful about hanging up his clothes at night. A matter of principle.

There was a canary yellow tie, a navy blue and white striped jacket, and white pants. Panic hit him again, this time a rushing wall of water that stopped his breathing and beat him down and destroyed his reason, and passed on leaving him whimpering again in witless terror.

He was back into The Dream again, all the comfort that came from the cozy explanation of being in a hotel destroyed in that instant of realization. THEY WERE SOMEONE ELSE'S CLOTHES. He had never owned clothes like that. He was in someone else's room, in someone else's bed, undressed. But it couldn't possibly be a dream. It was really happening. Suppose the owner came in, how could he explain it? How was he to get home without his clothes? How could he get out without being seen? And where was he? Which part of town? Which town?

And then he noticed the other clothes, also dropped carelessly on the floor. A green dress, a brassiere, and other things scattered round the room. And high heel shoes. He looked wildly round the room to find something, anything that would reflect reason. And only then did he realize that the other half of the bed was not as it should be. The pillow should have been plump and uncreased and unused, but it was flattened and crumpled and nearly off the bed. The bedclothes were thrown back, the undersheet creased and disarranged.

He nearly screamed at that moment, but gagged it in his throat and clenched his hands wildly onto the bedclothes for support. Oh god, oh god, he moaned, it gets worse and worse and worse. It's not possible. They can't have slept here, with me here too. They would have noticed me. Who are they anyway? They can't have left the house, they could be back at any moment. He forced his mind to stop racing, to stop thinking the unthinkable and sat listening. Nothing. But one thing became alarmingly certain. His bladder was uncomfortably full and would have to be relieved. And right away. He would have to get out of bed. But he must find something to put on. He couldn't risk someone coming back and catching him without clothes.

Getting out of bed took him a full minute. He dared not make a noise for fear of disturbing whoever might be outside, and every few moments he froze, listening, alert to dive back beneath the bedclothes if he should hear the slightest sound. At last he was standing on the carpet, head spinning and bladder aching, and looked about for a robe, anything to cover his embarrassment. But there was nothing other than the two sets of clothes on the floor, and either revulsion at wearing other people's cast-offs or reticence at taking another man's belongings deterred him from putting on the white trousers. There was only one thing to be done. He made a dash for the open door to the bathroom, suddenly aware as he did so that the man might already be there. Or worse, much worse, the woman. But there was no-one in the bathroom, and for the first time he relaxed. Then he went to the basin to wash his face, and looked into the large mirror above the counter.

That was when he screamed, a wild, anguished wail of horror and despair.

CHAPTER 4

The man staring back out of the mirror with terror filled eyes was someone else. Another person. Another face. An older face, with no mustache, the eyes red-rimmed, the mouth larger than his own but opened in his own reflected scream. These features were never his. He raised a hand to his face. The figure in the mirror did the same. He stooped and peered. The reflection stooped, and peered back. And yet it could not possibly be reflection. Not his reflection. He was Lawton Wainright, fine featured, slim. This man's face was well used, his body out of condition.

"Charlie, I heard a scream, are you alright?" The voice came from the bedroom, then the bathroom door opened.

This was what he had dreaded, being discovered without his clothes. But now there was no pride left, no self-respect, no embarrassment.

Still stooped, and with one hand still supporting himself on the vanity top, he turned toward the door. He hardly saw the brown curly hair, the owl-like glasses, the man's robe with the sleeves rolled back to the elbows. He saw only another human being, someone to cling to. And from the depth of his despair he held out one shaking hand to her, pleading.

"Help me, help me," he moaned.

"Charlie, darling, what's the matter?" She rushed to him, gathering him in her arms, lifting him and hugging him to her. "What is it, Baby, what's wrong?"

For a long time Lawton sobbed in Linda's arms while she held him, unable to understand his fear.

"What's hurting you, lover, tell me about it. It's alright, I'm with you now."

"Don't leave me," he begged her at last. "I don't know where I am."

"You've had a bad dream, darling. Everything's going to be all right now. You're at home. You're quite safe."

"It's not a dream," he sobbed. "This isn't my home. This isn't me. I don't know what's happened. It's horrible."

"Come into the bedroom," Linda said. "Come and sit on the bed and I'll fetch some coffee." She led him into the next room, holding him as if he might stumble and fall. And suddenly he was aware of his nakedness again.

"I can't stay like this. I don't know where my clothes are. Can you find me a robe?"

She fetched a robe from the closet, wondering about calling a doctor. Mental breakdown, she thought. What the hell do I do now? Lawton covered himself, and sat on the bed while she went out to fetch coffee. The crisis was past. The awful dread, the dread of being discovered, was gone. It was a comfort to be able to talk, to have someone near. The panic, too, was gone, leaving him drained and bewildered. This girl had called him Charlie, whoever Charlie was. He must look like Charlie, because certainly he didn't look like himself any more. What a pathetic idiot I must have looked, he thought. She must think I'm out of my mind. Perhaps I really am out of my mind? What other explanation can there be? She calls me Charlie, but I haven't the foggiest idea who this Charlie person is, or how I got here. Have I lost my memory? Amnesia? He clutched desperately at the explanation. Is this what amnesia's like? Not knowing where you are or how you got there?

He got up from the bed and crossed to the gilt-framed mirror. The basic features were not unlike his own. Or, at least, like the ones he used to have, because these were certainly his own now, he had to face that. No mustache, the hair cut shorter, a few years older. Been doing some hard living, judging by the eyes. And the taste in his mouth. Must have been away from Claire for quite a while. A few years? Did he walk out on her that night when they had the row? And start a new life?

Linda came in with two mugs of coffee on a tray. "You look better already," she said. "You're a bit hung over. The coffee might help."

"I feel a lot better," Lawton admitted. "I'm extremely grateful to you. I'm sorry I made such a fool of myself."

"I'm glad I was here to be with you, lover," She sat on the bed. "Come and sit, and drink your coffee. You must have been sleepwalking. It's supposed to be dangerous to wake up suddenly. You looked as if you were scared out of your skull when I found you."

"I was." Already he was feeling calmer. The shock had unnerved him. But now that he had an explanation, things didn't seem so bad. He wasn't crazy, anyway. He knew who he was, he could remember everything up to that last night with Claire. God! Claire must be out of her mind with worry. Or would she really care? He had to find out what he'd been doing since, and how long it was. It was going to be embarrassing sorting out a double life, but that was a rational problem, not like wondering whose bed he was in.

He sipped his coffee, with her arm protectively round him, wondering who she was, how he was going to explain to her that he had a wife. Presumably he'd been living with her? Good grief! He must have been sleeping with her. The thought aroused him, in spite of his worry.

She moved closer to him, resting her hand on his thigh. He was acutely conscious of the softness of her, her perfume exciting him. The earlier ghastly fear of embarrassment had passed, but now there was the shyness he had never been able to overcome, even as an adult. Even his earlier nakedness seemed less disturbingly intimate than such closeness to a strange girl, on a strange bed that they had apparently both been sharing.

She evidently expected some reaction. "I really do feel a lot better," he said. "I feel so guilty about this whole situation. I'm not really sure myself what's happened, but I think I can explain it." He stopped, catching sight of the blue and white striped jacket on the floor. It seemed less outrageous than when he had first noticed it. The room seemed more familiar, too. It was no longer so alien, so utterly strange. He could almost feel that he knew it, the prints on the wall, even the orange drapes.

"Linda Baby," he said. And stopped. That wasn't what he had meant to say. He never usually talked like that. But he had remembered her name.

"I think my memory's coming back," he said excitedly. "This is my apartment, right? I opened last night at the . . ."

"Tight Owl."

"Right. The Tight Owl." He jumped up from the bed and went quickly to one of the wide glass doors, opened it and stepped out onto the balcony. The parking lot below was familiar. He could pick out his own car. He knew the name of the street beyond. This was the Park Plaza. He was Charlie Chesney. Cheerful Charlie Chesney.

Linda came quietly behind him and put her arms round him. "That's what you meant when you said you didn't know where you were? You couldn't remember? You said, 'This isn't me.' I was so scared, I thought you'd had a breakdown or a stroke or something awful. You didn't even know me, did you?"

He turned round, and as if of their own will his hands opened the loose front of her robe, slipping inside to hold her. "I know you now, Linda Baby, every inch of you. Ten minutes ago I thought I'd die if anyone came in and found me starkers. And then you came in and it didn't seem to matter, you made everything all right. You are the greatest in the world, Honey."

"If you continue to strip me out here on the balcony I'm liable to be the greatest show in the world," Linda remonstrated. "You seem to be back to normal alright."

Lawton took his hands away quickly, blushing. "I really do apologize. I don't know what I was thinking of. Perhaps we'd better go inside."

"So that you can take advantage of me without anyone seeing. You'd like that, wouldn't you?"

"No, not at all," he stammered, blushing even more.

"You wouldn't? So now I'm to be spurned to my face. What's a girl got to do to get attention from you?"

He fled back into the bedroom. She followed, giggling mischievously. As he sat down on the bed she flung off the robe and posed in front of him, hands on hips. "What seems to be the trouble, Charlie?" she taunted.

"Don't do that!" he exclaimed. "You embarrass me." He looked down, away, anywhere but at the naked girl in front of him. The grin left her face. She dropped down beside him. "Poor baby," she said, putting her arms round him again. "You really aren't well. I've never seen you like this before."

He looked down at her body and quickly looked away, shaking his head in confusion. "I feel almost as if I've never seen you like that before. I wasn't used to this kind of thing. Claire never did anything like that."

"There must have been plenty who did, surely!" In spite of her concern an edge crept into her voice.

"I wasn't thinking of them. I was thinking of—before. When I was with Claire."

"Well who's Claire, then?"

"My wife."

"My gawd," she said, appalled. "Don't let the Press get hold of that. Cheerful Charlie Chesney with a wife! Where is she now?"

"I don't know. She must think I'm dead."

"Why? She must have been reading all about you. She'd have to be living in a convent not to."

"No, you see, before I—came here—I was Lawton Wainright. That's when we were married."

"You mean you changed your name?"

"I don't really know. I can't remember how it happened. I can't remember anything after the night we had the row."

"But just now it was this part you couldn't remember. You didn't even know me."

"I know. I think I must have lost my memory when I left Croftdown Road. I think I must have really hated her that night.

That's sometimes what causes amnesia, isn't it? Wanting to blot out something? And then something must have happened this morning. When I woke up all I could remember was the old life again. All this was gone."

"But it's all come back again now, hasn't it?" She was almost pleading, desperate for everything to be as it was.

"I think so. Except that everything's so mixed up. I don't know who I am. Which one, I mean. I seem to keep changing."

Linda got up, and began to straighten the bed. "You've had a pretty nasty shock. On top of a hangover that can't be good. Rest up for a while, Honey. Maybe you should get some sleep?"

He reached out and clutched her arm in alarm. "No, please! It was terrible when I woke up. You can't imagine how awful it is not to know where you are. I don't think I'll ever dare to sleep again."

She kissed him. "It won't happen again. You're all right now. Just rest up, even if you don't sleep. I'll go fix some breakfast. I'll leave the door open and you can call me if you don't feel good, O.K?"

"Thank you," he said, trying to smile. "Thank god you're not Claire."

"How d'you mean?"

"Looking after me like this. Sympathy. And understanding. Claire wasn't very good at that sort of thing."

"Bit of a bitch, you mean?"

For the first time since he had woken up he felt like laughing. "I suppose you could say that."

"Let's say that, then." She got a lot of satisfaction out of saying that.

When she looked in on him five minutes later he was asleep, leaning back against the headboard with 'Variety' still in one hand. She put breakfast preparations on hold, and started to freshen up the apartment. Charlie was not the tidiest of bachelors. Even though a housekeeper came in twice a week, he seemed to be able to produce disorder simply by being there. She smiled to herself. With the amount of sack time we've been putting in he shouldn't need rest now. Or have I been wearing him out?

It was about forty minutes later that he bellowed from the bedroom. "I thought you were supposed to be getting breakfast, woman. Am I supposed to stay here all day waiting for attention? What the b'jaisus are you doing out there?"

That sounds more like the old Charlie, she thought, and hurried into the bedroom. The bed was empty. He was just disappearing into the bathroom.

"You sound like your old self, Charlie," she called through the open doorway.

"And whose self would yous be wantin' me to sound like? Sure it's meself. In all me glory."

"Are you really alright?" She picked up his robe where he had dropped it on the floor. "You don't need me?"

"Sure I need you, Honey. Can't do without you. But right now if you don't get working on that breakfast and fix me something for this headache I'm liable to jump you and do unspeakably revolting things to you."

"Promises, always empty promises," she complained. "Leave the door open then, just in case. Are you going to take a shower?" She was answered by the sound of running water.

A few minutes later she took a brightly colored concoction in to him. "Sink this in one gulp," she ordered. "And don't get water in it."

"What is it?" he wanted to know, looking at it suspiciously and refusing to take it from her.

"Flaming onion. Fix your hangover."

"What's in it?"

"Sink it. I'll tell you after."

He looked at her a moment, then took the glass and drained it. "Jeeesus!" he exploded "That's terrible! That's a helluva thing to do to a man in my delicate condition. What is it, dynamite?"

"Raw egg, tomato juice, brandy, Worcestershire sauce, pepper, and Alka Selzer. And aspirin. How d'you feel?"

"Like I need a fire extinguisher. Can you see the flames coming out of the top of my head? Where did a nice girl like you learn a disgusting torture like that?"

"My mom used to fix them for Dad. Feel better?"

"You've got to be kidding! I'll never be the same again. Do you realize you've just blasted a hole clear through to the top of my head? I can sue you for this."

"So sue me," she said. "I'll get you on a morals charge."

"Morals? You don't have any morals. You've done nothing but corrupt me these last two weeks."

"One week," she corrected. "Five and a half days, to be exact."

"Good grief, I took you out of the gutter and now you think you can confuse me with facts?"

"If we're going to talk about facts," Linda replied loftily, with all the dignity of one whose left breast was being explored inside her robe by a wet hand, "may I remind you that I purchased you lock, stock and hangover for ten dollars and a quarter? And I had to pay the cab fare home on top of that. Plus a tip. The cab driver seemed to think I had a bargain."

"Sure you had a bargain. So I owe you ten and a quarter. Are you going to hold that against me all my life?"

"That might not be such a bad idea," she said quietly.

"Eh?"

"Never mind, Charlie. Just finish your shower and I'll have breakfast ready."

By the time he joined her in the kitchen, showered and shaved and smelling of Aramis, Linda had fresh coffee and croissants ready.

"Continental breakfast be alright?" she asked as he came in. "I don't know what you usually have Sundays."

"Just like any other day. Depends who's getting it."

Tactless, Linda thought. I suppose I'm only the latest incumbent but he doesn't have to rub it in. His way of making sure I don't feel too permanent, maybe.

Aloud she said, "Everything alright now? How's the hangover?"

"Linda Baby," he came up behind her and nuzzled her hair. "I may have to take you on as a permanent fixture. That flaming onion did wonders."

"What about the—other thing?"

"What other thing? The dream? Did I tell you about that? I know I woke up crying about something but the details have all gone, you know how it is with a dream. Anyway, more important things to think about right now."

"Like what?"

"The act. Got to make some changes before tomorrow." He sat opposite her at the table and helped himself to a croissant. "Got to have a meeting with the writers tonight and work it out."

"On Sunday?"

"Writers don't have Sundays, Baby. Not if they want to stay my writers. Say, I had an idea for a whole bunch of Reagan jokes. Like the one about the President's joke writer. How about the President hiring Groucho Marx to ghost write his autobiography?"

"Groucho's dead."

"That's why he's a ghost writer. You make a great straight man, Honey. Now see how this grabs you—this aviator who does sky-writing gets a bunch of ghost writers to write his copy, O.K?"

"So?"

"Ghost writers in the sky. O.K?"

"Maybe you'd better ask the writers, Charlie. I'm not an expert."

"Well Jeez, it can't be that bad. After the writers kick it around a bit. Try this one. Gorbachov says to Reagan, 'I was watchink one of your movies last week. Very goot.' Reagan says, 'If you like westerns wait till High Noon gets to Moscow,' O.K?"

Linda laughed, more at his intenseness than at the joke.

He threw up his hands. "So don't try to be a critic. Just stick to being a straight man."

"I'm not much help. I'm sorry," she apologized. "Tomorrow night I can sit out front and I promise I'll be your greatest fan."

"Sure, Honey. I'll have Merv sit with you and make sure you don't get any hassle. That reminds me, Sammy's got to make sure no-one gets up to leave during the monologue. It spoils the mood.

Last night there was this bunch of yahoos right up front, couldn't wait five minutes more. Woman with red hair, just like—Claire!"

He stopped, the awful realization hitting him like a punch between the eyes. He felt the blood drain from his face, his forehead grow clammy with the kind of cold sweat he used to get in The Dream. But this time it wasn't the horror of not knowing what was to come that frightened him.

This time it was what he knew that was so terrifying.

"What is it, my darling? Has it come back?" Linda reached across the table to take hold of his hands. "Tell me about it. What's happened?"

But he pulled away his hands to bury his face in them, his breath coming in great shuddering gasps. "Oh god, oh god, it's worse than before. I don't know what it means."

For a minute he sat with his face covered, gasping for breath, while Linda sat paralyzed, not knowing how to help. Then he looked up. "It was Claire. That was Claire out there, watching me."

Linda got up and moved round the table to stand beside him, letting him reach out to hold her painfully tight. She pressed his face against her, stroking his hair.

"It's all right, You don't have to go back to her. She was bound to see you some time."

He looked up at her. She saw the same despair that had been in his eyes before.

"It doesn't matter about Claire," he whispered. "It was me out there. With Claire. I saw him—me! I held out my hands to say sorry. I know it was me. I remember doing it. And it wasn't part of the old life. It was last night's show."

CHAPTER 5

By noon that day, Linda was convinced they needed a psychiatrist. His changes of mood frightened her. But it was his insistence that he had been in the Tight Owl, watching himself perform the night before, that unnerved her more. She had argued how impossible it was for him to be in two places at the same time, to be two people at the same time. Still he insisted he had gone home with Claire after the show, while she remembered all too clearly how he had gone to bed with her. And how good it had been. By two in the afternoon, she was even more convinced they needed help, but for a different reason. They had talked it through and through, round and round, over and over. He had recalled memories of his life with Claire, his university days with Jeff, even his childhood.

Yet, as the effect of his most recent shock wore off, the Chesney exuberance returned. And as the dominance of the Chesney personality increased, so the Lawton memories seemed to recede. The only explanation seemed to be that his subconscious was fabricating the whole complex structure of the Lawton persona that was so convincing. And if this were so he needed help, badly.

By four that afternoon, the old Charlie cheerfulness seemed to be quite restored.

"So you think my subconscious is making things up?" he said. "Seems the best explanation yet, and not nearly so scary as the other ideas. Maybe I can train it to make up jokes. Or write a new act. Maybe the two of us can go on as a double act. Chesney and Wainright, the Double Identity. How about that?"

She tried to get into the mood with him. "He may not go for that. He may insist on Wainright and Chesney."

"So I'll get him exorcised. That'll fix him."

That may not be so far from the truth, Linda thought miserably. But it seems best not to talk about psychiatrists and the can of worms that idea might open up. He can never do the show tomorrow if he's still having these fits of the horrors, and he has to meet the writers tonight. So maybe it's time to change the subject while he's riding high.

"Time for a drinky-poo," she announced brightly.

"Time for a WHAT?"

"Drinky-poo. We've had some shocks today, and we've been on a coffee jag all day. Time we had a pick-me-up."

"I must be in worse shape than I thought," he said, "when you have to remind me to reach for the bottle. Make mine a ginny-poo, Lindy-poo."

While Linda fixed the drinks, her mind drifted to practical things. For four of the past five evenings, she had dashed home from the ad agency where she was an account executive, to shower and change and dash out again to meet Charlie. Yesterday, she had spent the whole day at the club while he rehearsed and made last minute changes to the act. So there were dirty dishes at home, laundry to be done, and the garbage to be put out.

"Charlie," she said suddenly, "I've just got to get back to the apartment some time today. I think maybe I'll go while you're with the writers."

"No Baby, don't do that." She could hear the alarm in his voice. "I want you to stay with me."

"But Charlie, I've got so much to do. And I need clothes. Look at me, I'm still in your robe. I've nothing to wear about the place even."

"Please, Linda." Damn! she thought, I've killed his high mood.

"The way this thing keeps coming and going worries me," he said. "I need you with me in case anything else happens."

"But you'll be with the writers, Honey."

"They can't help. They don't know. And I can't tell them. You're the only one who knows. Help me through today, please Linda."

"Of course, my darling. I should have thought." He was right. There was no way he should be left alone while he was so frightened. "We can both go back to the apartment after the meeting. Will that be alright?"

By the time they left to meet the writers, he was in high spirits. Nothing happened to spoil his mood, and it was a hilarious session, something quite outside Linda's experience. Even the jokes that had seemed so flat a few hours before had Linda crying with laughter.

"I told you they needed kicking around a bit," he reminded her. "The jokes, not the writers. These boys are good. They could get a laugh out of a laundry list. Only don't tell them, it's bad for a writer's ego. And my bank account."

The evening passed with no hint of further crisis. At Linda's apartment, she set him to doing the kitchen chores while she undressed and put her underwear into the washing machine with the contents of a nearly full laundry hamper. As she hunted through dresser drawers and sorted out clothes, he came into the room.

"I've never known any girl spend so much time out of her clothes," he exclaimed.

"This must be the first time you've given me the chance to take them off by myself. Have you finished your work in the kitchen, Cinderella?"

"Yes, Stepmother dear." He dropped a curtsey.

"Well," Linda said, "I'd better think of something else to keep you busy for a while."

"No problem." he grinned, and slowly took off his jacket. "I've already thought of something. You're going to enjoy this."

It was nearly midnight when they arrived back at Chesney's apartment.

"I've got to work tomorrow," Linda stated firmly. And it's been one hell of a day today, she thought, but kept it to herself because he seemed to have forgotten the earlier experiences. "So it's bedtime for Linda. How about you?"

"The way this woman harps on bed!" he exclaimed, borrowing from Noel Coward. "If I turned down an invitation like that my conscience would never recover."

"Sleep!" she said. "That's what the invitation is about."

* * *

Lawton slept right through till nearly seven the next morning, waking with the dread already uppermost in his mind. Was there another horror in store?

"Linda?" he whispered, and reached out for her. But the bed beside him was empty. The sound of a radio came faintly from outside the door. She's making coffee, he thought hopefully, but lay for a while not ready to face the possibility of more terror outside the security of the bedclothes. When he opened his eyes to the familiar bedroom he could feel the relief course through himself. No nightmare. No waking to a strange environment. Please god it's all over. Linda must have been as worried as I was.

But suddenly he knew that indeed it was not all over. Suddenly he recognized the pictures on the walls for what they were—framed cut-outs from fashion magazines. He saw the pale blue scalloped drapes, the cluttered dressing table. Twisting his head, he saw the gold satin headboards, two of them, one for each of the twin beds. And he knew where he was. Dear god, he thought, don't make me go through it all again. Yesterday he had been trying to get back to sleep so that he could wake up in the house at Croftdown Road, yet now he almost felt he wanted it to be at the Park Plaza apartment. Had he come back home, or was he still Chesney? Who was he? He knew what he must do. The mirror over the dressing table was only feet away. And yet he was reluctant to know. It was the sound of the radio that made up his mind for him. He dared not have Claire come back before he knew for sure. With these pale blue drapes he knew it must be Claire, and yet somehow he wanted it to be Linda. But how could it be Linda? This was his nightmare, not hers.

Reluctantly he threw back the bedclothes, and sat on the side of the bed. Not naked this time, anyway. And they were his own pajamas. His? Lawton Wainright's. Good grief! He'd only been away a day and already Lawton Wainright seemed like a stranger. Or had he been away? Could he have spent yesterday here without remembering it? He had to know. And yet still he hesitated. Who did he want to be? All he knew was that he had an empty longing for Linda.

He crossed to the dressing table, and looked. And as the face of Lawton Wainright looked back at him the duality seemed to slip from him. Of course he was Lawton Wainright! Why should he have doubted it? He was at home. Yesterday's episode had been—what? A fantasy dreamed up in his subconscious just as Linda had suggested it was. Only it was Chesney who was the dream character, not Wainright. But was Linda only a dream character as well?

Snap out of it! he thought. We can go round and round like this forever. It's Monday morning, Claire goes to dancercise class, there's a meeting with the Board this afternoon. And right now it's time to shower and shave. What's the time? It was seven thirty. On Mondays, Claire usually left him to sleep till she went out, because the museum was closed. This was officially his day off in place of Saturday. Saturday was a normal working day at the museum. With a last quick look in the mirror, he opened the bedroom door, the events of the previous day fading to a vague shadow at the back of his mind.

As he came out of the bathroom twenty minutes later, Claire came up and presented her face to be kissed. It was not an affectionate gesture, but a tribute she considered her due, particularly if there were other people about. "I'm on my way. You don't need the car till one, right? You feeling better today?"

"Lots thank you, dear," he replied, wondering how he was supposed to be feeling yesterday. He was not ready to admit to Claire that yesterday was a blank apart from half-formed hallucinations flitting through his memory. What had he done yesterday? What had he said?

"You were in a shocking state yesterday," she said accusingly. "I was worried sick. I've never seen you with a hangover like that. You were saying the most ridiculous things, I thought you'd gone out of your mind. And you were very rude, too. I had to leave, you were so gross."

He could think of nothing else to say but, "I'm sorry dear. I have to be at the Board meeting by two. Have a nice morning."

During the next two days, it was as if a curtain had dropped in front of Sunday's trauma. Something was in his mind to be remembered, he was aware of that, but it was like a dream that refused to be recalled, and he quickly forgot its very existence. There was a budget fight to be faced with a hard-nosed faction of the Board. And he had to do something about Miss Saunders. She was altogether too lacking in—what was the word? Modesty, really. It just wouldn't do for a place like the museum. He could take the fight with the Board in his stride, but Miss Saunders' nipples were quite another matter. Certainly nothing he could take in his stride. Perhaps he could leave confronting them—confronting the subject—till he had talked to Jeff. Jeff might have an idea how to broach the matter tactfully.

There was something else on his mind that he found difficult to define. Miss Saunders'—er—bust, seemed to make him conscious of a vague emptiness, an aching sense of longing as if for something treasured that was lost. And yet, if he tried to analyze it and recall it, nothing remained. On Tuesday night, it became so strong that he almost trapped it. He was reading in bed, waiting for Claire to come to bed after a lengthy beautification drill. She liked him to stay awake with his reading light on until she came to bed. And then the nightly ritual seldom varied. She would settle herself in the other twin bed, then lean across to let him kiss her cheek. This time, as he dutifully kissed the proffered cheek, the scent of her face cream was so evocative that memory flooded back. The perfume, subtle but arousing. A body warm and close beside him. Arms that held him comfortingly. And a voice that murmured, "Poor baby."

"Linda," he whispered to himself. "Oh Linda!" But instantly it was gone, the warmth and the comfort, and, yes, the sense of love. And he was left with just the meaningless name and a nameless empty longing.

He dreamed about her that night. It seemed as if the dream continued all night long, her arms holding him from behind, her body close against his. And in the morning she was there. So were the orange drapes, and the sunshine streaming in through the wide glass doors with the balcony outside. But above all she was there, just as she had been in The Dream. This time there was no terror. The terror had come with not knowing where he was, with the awful realization of his nakedness in a strange place, with not knowing who might discover him. This time he knew where he was, and the nakedness was something quite pleasant. And he knew who was going to discover him.

Linda was still sleeping, her arms so tightly about him that he could hardly twist inside her embrace. As he kissed her eyes, her nose, her hair, he realized how much he had hungered for her. Yet he could not bring himself to kiss her mouth. That seemed unfaithful to Claire. Besides, he hardly knew Linda, and it seemed wrong to take advantage of her while she slept. After all, she was Charlie's girl really. And then he smiled to himself. These were strange thoughts for a man in bed with a woman.

As he kissed her mouth she stirred, responding with increasing warmth. His hand explored the smoothness of her.

"That's a nice way to wake up," she said sleepily.

"I've been dreaming about you all night," he said. "Or maybe I've really been with you all night." He drew back to look into her eyes. "There was an emptiness without you. And now I've come back. Do you mind?"

CHAPTER 6

Linda drew away from him on the pillow to look at his face. "Oh-oh, so it's happened again has it? How does it feel this time?"

"There seems to be no trauma this time," Lawton answered seriously. "And I have you to come to. I still find it impossible to be sure which is the real thing and which is the dream, but the abject terror is gone."

"Well don't start to enjoy it too much," Linda admonished him. "You're going to turn me into a basket case if this goes on. Have you any idea what it's like to wake up in the morning and see the same old face but not know who's inside?"

He was seized with guilt immediately. "I'm terribly sorry, Linda. I was being thoughtless. And I've no right to expect you to want to see me."

"You've no right to put your hand where it is, either," she chided. "We haven't been properly introduced."

He drew back his hand as if it had been stung. "I'm really terribly sorry . . ." he began, but she interrupted him.

"I was kidding, silly." She drew his head toward her on the pillow and kissed him softly,

"I'm terribly embarrassed about all this," he said when she let him go.

"That's what you said Sunday morning."

"That was a different kind of embarrassment. What I mean is, I feel as if I'm here under false pretenses. I hardly know you, and I'm behaving as if I have a right to be in bed with you."

"If I don't jump out of bed screaming for Mother, then you can assume I'm not objecting very strongly," she assured him.

"And as for not knowing me, your left hand's getting to know me pretty intimately again right now."

He drew back his hand again with a gasp. "I do apologize, really," he stammered, and moved away from her. "I don't know what's come over me, I've never done anything like that before. Look, I think I'd better get dressed."

"You mustn't take me so seriously, lover," Linda said, following him across the bed. "I'm so used to kibitzing with—Charlie."

"I find it so difficult to know just how to behave," Lawton said. "I'm rather a reserved person normally, and suddenly I find myself in bed with another man's girl. What if he were to come in now? It would be dreadful."

Linda sat up on one elbow. "He won't come in now," she said. "Didn't you talk to Claire about all this?"

"Hardly at all. We don't talk much. Actually, I think she'd rather criticize than talk. She said I had a hangover on Sunday. She wouldn't tell me what happened, but she said I was gross."

"I can imagine that." Linda took his hand. "What do you think was happening here yesterday? And Monday, while you were away."

"That's something that worries me, Linda. I don't know how to say this without hurting you. But—my life at Croftdown Road is the real one, I'm sure. It's been going on for years. So—does that mean all of this is something my subconscious has invented? And you too?"

Linda gave a little shriek of laughter. "Do you really think you could have made me up? Am I the sort of girl your mind would have invented? Am I your dream girl?"

Lawton blushed. "As a matter of fact, I think you are. I've never known anyone like you, but I think I must have always wanted to."

"I'm flattered, really," Linda said, and put her face close to Lawton's till their noses touched. "But let me tell you I'm no hallucination. My life's been going on for years, too. Feel me. Hold me. Do you really think I disappear when you're not here?"

He had no answer.

"Listen," she said seriously. "I've got something to tell you. I thought you might have worked it out already. Charlie and I talked it through Monday morning, while it was still fresh in his mind. Now listen. When you came here Sunday morning Charlie somehow got switched with you. He was at Croftdown Road. With Claire."

"Poor Charlie!" Lawton said quietly.

"Claire thought he was you. He went through just the same sort of hell you went through, not knowing where he was, who he was. It was probably even worse for poor Charlie. Claire was absolutely rotten to him. Now, do you see what that means?"

"It's impossible. It means—we're exchanging personalities. Or bodies. It's like science fiction. It's absurd."

"Whatever it is, it means it's not in your mind. Both of you are having the same thing happen. It means you're not making up the whole Croftdown Road bit, or this. And you're not making me up either."

Lawton was still adjusting to the idea of Charlie taking his place at Croftdown Road. "You mean Charlie's there again now? While I'm here?"

"I guess so. I feel sort of guilty, as if I should be there to help him through it. It doesn't sound as if he'll get much understanding from Claire."

Lawton whistled. "Poor devil! It must have been awful for him. I think I'd have gone out of my mind without you here. Claire's probably giving him the silent treatment just about now."

"What's that?"

"She won't talk. There's no way you can get through to her. What did Charlie think of her?"

"He says she needs smacking and screwing every day for a month, and heavy on the smacking. He says you obviously haven't been training her properly."

"He's probably right. But I could never hit a woman. I just hate confrontations of any sort."

"You mean you don't have rows with Claire?"

"I'm afraid so. Except for last Saturday night. Something seemed to break then, and I shouted at her, and I hated her for making me shout at her. Perhaps I was already beginning to change."

Linda made a sudden decision, and flung back the bedclothes. "Coffee," she said, and stood up. Lawton gazed enthralled at the unabashed way she stood in front of him, showing off her body. If only Claire could have been like this, he thought, instead of prudish and selfish. My own fault for marrying her, I suppose. But then I didn't know anyone could be like this. Chesney's right, she probably needs to be shown she can't have everything her own way. But I couldn't hit her. Might be fun to give her a good spanking, though.

"I'm going to put the coffee on." Linda seemed unconscious of the effect her body was having on him. "I seem to have done nothing but talk about this thing for days. First you, then Charlie, now you again. I'm having to play den-mother to both of you." A sudden thought struck her. "Do you know, if I'd walked home instead of taking a cab I never would have got mixed up in this."

Lawton looked at her blankly. "I'm sorry?"

"Never mind," she said. "I was just thinking of all the trouble you can buy for ten and a quarter. Do you think you can learn to live with this?"

"I think I already have," he said. "This morning when I woke up I felt as if I'd come home. I can live with it if you're part of it."

"I said live with this, not live with me. You're tit-hungry and that usually colors a man's perceptions. I'm not talking about you moving in with me every so often in Charlie's place. It's not that simple. This is the third time you've switched, and we'd better face up to it, there's no reason why this should be the last time. It could go on for a long time. So we've all got problems, all three of us."

Linda was in the kitchen when Lawton came in to her with a new thought. "Does this mean Charlie has to take my place at the museum today?"

"Well, I guess so, unless you manage to do another change before then."

"But that's dreadful!" He was appalled. "He doesn't know anything about it. How will he manage?"

"About the same way you'll manage with Charlie's show tonight, I guess."

Lawton looked at her aghast. "You can't mean it? It's absolutely preposterous. I couldn't do it. I've never done anything like that before. This is terrible. We're going to ruin each other's careers."

She laughed at his consternation, and gave the knife another twist. "That's not the half of it. You're on the Mike Flynn Show at two this afternoon. I feel like an appointments secretary."

"This is nothing to joke about." Lawton slumped into a chair. "This is just dreadful. I couldn't pretend to be Charlie, they'd see through me in a minute."

Linda put a coffee mug on the table in front of him. "Do you remember meeting the writers on Sunday?"

"What writers?"

"That's what I thought. Once you were settled in here you seemed to slide right into Charlie's personality. It was like you really were Charlie. You talked like him, you acted like him. You went to meet the writers and made changes to the show, and they didn't have any idea it wasn't Charlie."

"Perhaps it really was Charlie. How do you know we hadn't changed back?"

"Because when something happened to remind you of Claire, Lawton was right there showing through. Charlie seems to have been the same. After he'd settled in he didn't remember a thing, and you told me Claire just thought he had a hangover."

"So I've got to spend the day hoping Charlie's personality sort of takes me over? Sounds like a recipe for disaster." Another thought struck him. "What do I do about clothes? I can't wear Charlie's things."

"Honey, you can't stay indoors for ever. And you can't go out balls naked. I'm sorry, I'm embarrassing you again. But there's nothing else here for you to wear. I'm afraid we've both got to get used to the idea—this is Charlie's body, so while you're using it you are Charlie. Or am I supposed to call you Lawton on Monday, Wednesday and Friday and Charlie on Tuesday, Thursday and Saturday?"

"I feel like an interloper," he said miserably. "Using Charlie's apartment, and his clothes. And his girl."

"I don't know about using Charlie's girl," Linda remonstrated, "but it occurs to me I'm practically a virgin as far as Lawton Wainright is concerned."

"I'm sorry?" He was mystified.

"We wake up in bed together, and you haven't laid me. I kiss you and you say it embarrasses you. I don't even know what this Wainright character's like in the sack."

"Linda, really!" He had never considered himself a prude, but this directness startled him.

Immediately, Linda was contrite. "I'm sorry, my darling. You're just going to have to get used to my kidding. But seriously, it's not easy trying to live with a man you don't really know." She got up from her chair and went round the table to him, standing between him and the table. "May I sit down?"

"Oh please," he said, not sure what she meant.

"Thank you." She leaned over him, opening the skirt of her robe and sitting astride his knees, her arms loosely round his neck.

"Listen to me again. Any moment now you could start forgetting all about Lawton, and slip into Charlie's personality. Or for all I know you might up and do a switch and go back to Claire, though that always seems to happen overnight. Now, hold me close. That's better." She lowered her head to kiss him, exploring his mouth gently with her tongue, and then inviting him to explore her. The gentle, lingering softness was so unlike Claire's passive rigidity, when she was in the mood at all. There was enticement, and giving, and warmth, and promise. And above all tenderness, the tenderness he must have hungered for without realizing what it was he missed.

His hands held her, exploring, responding to the soft warmth of her body. She lifted her head, and pulled apart the top of her robe, knowing the shyness was gone from him at last.

"We may be seeing a lot of each other, my darling," she whispered. "And you can't go on for ever being embarrassed and guilty and apologizing for everything. We've got to get to know each other. That's if you want me to stay here with you. This is your apartment, you know."

For reply he could only hold her more urgently, pressing his face against her as if he would become a part of her.

A half an hour later she stirred in his arms, sighing with contentment.

"A whole two hundred thousand dollar apartment, and you have to lay me on the kitchen floor," Lawton complained.

"Well, I mopped it last night," Linda countered. "Besides, you weren't about to move into the next room. You were impatient, to say the least. Hey, that was the sort of remark Charlie makes. It looks like I just got to know you in time."

"It's a very strange sensation," Lawton said. "I know I'm Lawton Wainright, and yet I have no qualms about the Mike Flynn Show. I know just how I'm going to handle it."

"How about tonight's show?"

"No problem. I don't have to think about it. I just know it's all right there in the old Chesney miracle box. Funny, though, the old Lawton persona's getting to be more and more of a stranger."

"Not to me he's not. I said we should get to know each other better, and we sure did that. In spades. I didn't expect you to know anything about such perverted activities."

He grinned at her, a little proudly. "Read about them in the Khama Sutra. East Indian History, second year.

Never thought I'd try them out, though. Say, what's the time? I've got things to do before the talk show."

"Nearly eight thirty," Linda said. "I'm going to call in sick again. I think I should come with you again today, just in case."

"Sure, Baby. Only don't let them sucker you into talking off the record. Flynn'd give his left nut for a story like this."

She got up to go to the phone, but he caught her arm. "Linda Baby. Linda, dear Linda. I'm getting rather mixed up. Mixed signals.

But—before Chesney gets too many ideas into my head I want to tell you something. Just in case this whole thing blows up and ends as suddenly as it began. I want you to know I love you so very much, so much more than anyone I've ever known."

"I think I'm in love with you, too, my darling. That's why I made a play for you this morning, before you could change on me." She bent down to kiss him, aware as she did so that she was falling in love with someone who only existed for a few hours at the time. Wondering, too, whether she was being unfaithful to Charlie, even though she had never been in love with him. As she crossed to the phone, she had the wild thought that possibly she could track Lawton to Croftdown Road, where his real life was.

But what if it turned out there was no such place? No such real life? No such person as Lawton Wainright?

CHAPTER 7

Charles Delano Chesney, Junior, needed a drink. Badly. His father, Charles Delano Chesney, Senior, would certainly never have approved of such a craving, particularly so early in the morning. But then his father, who was named for a Democratic president and raised in an ultra Republican family environment, always believed fervently that self-control was a virtue and deferred gratification built character. Charles Chesney Junior also had strong beliefs. He believed that self-control was all right for those who liked it, and delayed gratification was a load of codswallop and no good for anyone. And that a noggin in need was a lifesaver indeed. This morning, Charlie felt every justification for craving a drink. At the precise moment that Linda McClusky was waking to the tentative kisses of Lawton Wainright, Claire Wainright was finding it necessary to chastise the man she believed to be her husband.

She had already exhausted the 'You can't think much of me to subject me to this kind of humiliation day after day' theme, and was well into 'It's downright despicable for a man in your position to be a secret drinker.'

Charlie could have found this last slur easier to bear if he had been as hungover as Claire insisted he was. Indeed, at that very moment, he would even have welcomed a hangover. As it was, the unnerving experience of waking unexpectedly in another man's bed, to face the early morning vapors of another man's wife, was unlikely to bring out the best in any man, especially a confirmed bachelor accustomed to choosing his bed companions reasonably carefully.

As he headed for the bathroom, less out of need than to get out of range of the harangue from the bedroom, he considered his earlier assessment of Claire. Screwing she probably needed, he thought, but in her present mood he was certainly not the man to do it. Though what he'd seen of her frame inside that thing she called a nightdress looked passable enough. Perhaps some other time? And spanking she certainly needed, but some sense of sympathy for the nebulous Lawton whom he had never met deterred him from any course that might make Lawton's life even more difficult.

He passed by the bathroom door, and went on into the living room. The liquor cabinet hardly deserved the name, he decided. Evidently maintained for the benefit of unexpected guests. But Famous Grouse was too good for guests, unexpected or otherwise, and he poured himself a generous glass. He passed on into the kitchen. A little ice could do the Scotch no harm, and he needed the extra bite. By the time he arrived at the bathroom, he felt at least prepared to face whatever ghastliness the day might produce. The terrible dreamlike horror of his first visit on Sunday was past. He had some idea of what he had to face, and he reasoned that if this could happen to him twice in four days, it was more than likely it could happen again. So there was every reason to put on the Chesney smile, get a good belt or two under the belt and make the best of an impossible situation. Particularly since there was no point in trying to explain to Claire. That way led to a straitjacket, and he might never get home again.

His mind flashed back to Linda. She must be the ninety-ninth this year, he thought, and yet there's something a little bit special about her. Could be just that she happened to be there when I needed her. But I wish she'd happen to be right here, I could do with a bit of sympathy and understanding right now. And nooky. Probably giving all the sympathy and understanding to that craphead Wainright. And nooky, too, blast him.

However, the Scotch seemed to be making the outlook a little more rosy. The Scotch and his natural cheerfulness. He didn't call himself Cheerful Charlie Chesney for nothing. Already he felt more confident, more assured in his assumed character of Lawton Wainright.

The mustache is a good touch, he felt, as he carefully shaved round it. Gives a little character. Takes away a little of the unsureness when I smile. Almost an Errol Flynn smile. Certainly Miss Saunders seems to like it. Really must discourage her advances, though. They're so blatant. On the other hand, why? She's some cute chick. Are those knockers really real? Definite potential there. Not the right way to think about one's staff, though. Very poor office management. Probably the best way would be to discuss the whole thing with her. Over a gin and tonic after office hours? No, of course not. Explain that a secretary shouldn't get a crush on the boss. Sure would like to know if they're real, though.

By the time he was dressed, he could feel the Wainright personality trying to eclipse his own, just as it had on Sunday. But he couldn't let Chesney sink without trace in this miasma of establishment conformity. Some parting gesture had to be made, even if only for his self esteem.

There was a small closet by the front door where a few tools were kept. He could picture them as if he had used them before. Quickly he fetched a small screwdriver and made for the bathroom, fearful that Lawton might be able to divert him before he got there. Claire was in the shower, her shape showing indistinctly through the frosted glass door. Stupid idea, frosting shower doors, he thought. Let's have a look at what I have to come home to tonight. He slid back one door.

Claire glared at him, amazed that he should invade her privacy. For the first time ever. He put one hand to his ear and mimed.

"Telephone, dear," he shouted over the noise of the shower. "For you."

Not bad at all, he thought as he frankly surveyed all of Claire that was showing through the streaming water. Cute little buns. I could have been stuck with something far worse.

Claire turned off the shower, reached for a towel and held it in front of herself.

"Telephone," he said urgently.

"Well can't you take a message? I can't answer the phone like this, can I?"

"Thought you'd want to answer it yourself. Mayor's office. Might be a cocktail party or something."

"Well don't get in the way then." She put a wet hand on the shoulder of his suit, nearly overbalancing him in her haste to get out of the shower, and ran through the bathroom door. Charlie neatly grabbed the towel as she passed, holding one corner so that it slipped from her and he was able to admire the retreating derriere in its entirety.

"What you need is a few sharp whacks across that little backside," he said quietly as he took the screwdriver out of his pocket.

The handle of the bathroom door was the kind that was held onto a shaft through the door by a single screw. He quickly removed the screw, and put it on the shelf over the vanity. Lawton would be needing it later. Once the screw was removed, the knob on the inside of the door could be pulled off. Or, better still, the outside knob and the whole shaft could be removed from outside the door. Chances were, when Claire rushed back into the bathroom and slammed the door, the whole works would slide out and end up on the floor outside. If it didn't, it could so easily be assisted. And when Claire found no one on the phone, she most certainly would be slamming the door.

He walked quickly to the door of the den to listen. Claire was talking to the switchboard at City Hall, trying to find out who had been calling her. He had plenty of time. There was a jug of orange juice in the fridge. And a bottle of vodka in the liquor cabinet. Half and half should be a good mixture. Claire would be locked in the bathroom for a long time, and she'd need something to sustain her. He put the jug on the shelf by the mirror where she would be bound to notice it. By the time he came home she should be feeling no pain.

He heard the phone slammed down, and waited by the bathroom door as she ran out of the den, oblivious of her interesting nudity in her fury. "What did they want, dear?" he asked innocently.

"They hung up," she spat at him through her tears. "You certainly took your time telling me. And don't be late home tonight, I shall need the car to go round to Celia's."

Charlie smiled, and let his eyes play over her. "You won't be needing the car, Baby," he told her. "I've got plans for you this evening. Something you'll enjoy."

The bathroom door slammed behind her. The handle with its shaft shot out with such speed he almost failed to catch it. He heard a quiet thump from inside the bathroom as the inner handle fell onto the bathroom rug. Claire would not have heard it.

"I'm leaving now," he called through the door.

"Goodbye dear." Let the bitch cool off for a few hours!

* * *

"Morning Mr. Topham." Charlie strode up the broad stone steps to where the uniformed Head Commissionaire stood at parade rest, waiting and ready to open the front door of the museum with that pomp and circumstance that only Commissionaires can give to such an event.

"Morning, Sah." Obadiah Topham was once a British Sergeant Major, and therefore was always a Sergeant Major, and desired all to be aware of it.

There was something undefinably pleasant about standing at the top of a broad flight of steps, Charlie decided. Must be almost like being on a stage. And the sun was shining full on him just like a spotlight. He had always entered the museum by this same front door in this very same way, and yet today there seemed to be something extra special about the routine, as if he was about to give a performance to the people passing by below. But he was an archaeologist, not an actor. He had always carried this same neatly furled umbrella, hoping he would never need to unroll it, but today he had to suppress an urge to engage the Head Commissionaire in swordplay, and force him step by step down to the sidewalk where he would run him through the heart.

"How are the bombs, Mr. Topham?" he asked, more to prolong the moment than out of any real interest.

"Sah?"

"The bombs, Mr. Topham. Haven't found any left behind by terrorists or tourists or anyone?"

"No Sah. No bombs, Sah."

"Well, that's all right then, Mr. Topham. Don't want a repetition of that National Bank incident, do we?"

"What incident was that, Sah?"

"Commissionaire found a package by the vault. Smelled of sulphur. Ticking noise inside. Called the bomb squad. Detonated a ham on rye, two hard boiled eggs and an alarm clock."

"Very amusing, Sah. But why would anyone bring an alarm clock in a lunch bag, Sah?"

"Just to make it a better story, Mr. Topham." Good straight man, Topham! Charlie opened the door for himself, for the first time in eight years, and quite spoiled the Head Commissionaire's day. He looked about him as he crossed the vestibule. It certainly was an imposing old pile, with its marble pillars and beautiful curved staircase. On the wall at the top of the stairs, staring out superciliously at anyone ascending the stairs, was the head of a large moose. He had suffered this creature's scorn at least ten times each week for the past eight years, his memory told him. Suffered impotently, for what can one do to get even with a stuffed moose? It was time, he decided, that something was done to demonstrate that a moose had a limited function in society, one that did not include upstaging the boss.

In the top drawer of his desk, at the rear left corner, was a black comb. It was always there, just in case he should be caught in a windstorm, or even a draft, so that he could tidy his hair. This was in addition to the one in his briefcase and another in the breast pocket of his suit. He was particular about a well-groomed appearance. Beside the comb there should be a spare pair of glasses. And in the right hand corner was a cigar in a plastic case that had been presented to him nearly three years before by a happy father. It would be very dry by now. These three items and a chair were all he needed. Listening first for any sound of office staff approaching from the floor below, or Miss Saunders in the next office, he placed the chair directly under the offending head, climbed onto it, and improved the facial appearance of the beast. He got down from the chair and stepped back to look. Groucho Moose! It would be instructive to listen to the comments of the visitors. Customers, Miss Saunders called them.

Ah yes. Miss Saunders. She deserved more attention than he had given her since she became his secretary. He had always prided himself on being an excellent administrator. You didn't earn a Doctorate in Archaeology without a good grounding in Business Management, after all. But a first class administrator might possibly have been a tad more approachable. He had tended to keep her very much at arms' length. Anything closer could almost be classed as body contact.

He opened the desk drawer again and took out his personal telephone directory, the calculator, dictionary, Thesaurus and calendar, and placed them neatly on the desk. There were only three items listed on the calendar. The Chairman of the Board was due at eleven to discuss, off the record, ways of forcing the budget past the recalcitrant faction. Rosemary Gwynn refused to be called the Chairperson. She found that too impersonal, and, he suspected, insufficiently authoritative. She was a well built, handsome spinster of estimated age about thirty-five. Well built in the way of a Spanish galleon, high prowed, well proportioned and efficient. Handsome in that her looks were too domineering for any more feminine epithet. And spinster only because her superior armament discouraged most men-o'-war from lying alongside. She was accustomed to having her way, both on and off the Board, by vocal intimidation and the frequent expedient of crying Foul. She could invoke Feminine Equality, Male Chauvinism, Roberts Rules of Order and Discrimination Against the Gentler Sex with bewildering lack of logic. And usually won her point.

At two every Wednesday, Lawton was in the habit of conducting through the Egyptian Room a class from one or other of the local high schools. He normally had little contact with the public, but Jeff was Vice Principal of one of the schools, and Jeff could be very persuasive.

At four, he was due to give the Elgin Memorial lecture to the Historical Society. *Archaeology in America* should take no longer than two hours, including the opening address and question period.

He always made a quick tour of the premises first thing each morning, noting on a pad any item that needed attention. After that he would have time to go over his lecture notes before Miss Gwynn arrived. Mizz Gwynn, as she insisted. He took a small note pad and pencil from the desk drawer and opened the office door.

Good gracious! I'd forgotten all about Groucho Moose! He was shocked. I can't really believe I did that. Most unbecoming. But it's awfully good. The old place needs a little light-heartedness. He strode quickly through the galleries, so familiar with every detail that a misplaced notice or a faulty exhibit would have caught his eye instantly. He found no problems worth noting on the pad, and arrived back at his office shortly after nine o'clock.

But in the Classical Room Apollo's hand now cupped Diana in a startlingly intimate way.

CHAPTER 8

He had hardly sat at his desk when the door from Miss Saunders' office burst open with all the urgency of an Act of God.

"Good morning Doctor Wainright I'm sorry I forgot to knock is there any dictation this morning?" Miss Saunders appeared in front of his desk as if released from a spring, shaking the hair back from a face that bubbled with eagerness. As did her bust, Charlie noted with interest. Metaphorically speaking, of course.

"Not at the moment thank you, Miss Saunders," he said, transferring his gaze with an effort to the lecture notes in front of him. "A little later I may want you to make some changes in these notes you typed for me."

"Weren't they alright? Did I make some mistakes?"

"They are perfectly alright. It's just that I may be making some changes. But there's something else I want to discuss with you."

"Is it something wrong? I have been making out alright, haven't I?"

"I have no way of knowing whether or not you're making out, Miss Saunders. I'm only concerned with what goes on during working hours." Charlie looked up at a wide black belt cinched tightly round a tiny waist, a pink sweater stretched almost beyond the limits of safety, and—oh my god, they can't be real!

How far should I push him, Miss Saunders wondered. There's got to be some fire under that ice.

"I should have spoken to you about this before," Charlie continued. "But I didn't want to discourage you during your first week."

"Is it my shorthand, Doctor Wainright? I could work it up for you."

"You do, Miss Saunders. That is to say you could." Charlie was losing his cool. Maintain a pleasant manner, he quoted to himself. Anger betrays lack of self-control. "But that's not what I'm talking about. At least, not working up your shorthand."

"My typing, then?"

"Will you belt up, you dumb broad!" Charlie said in the same quiet restrained tone, vaguely surprised to hear such an expression coming from his own mouth. "I don't give a fish's tit about your typing." (Got him on the move now, thought Miss Saunders.)

"I'm talking about your natural exuberance." (Or would protuberance be more to the point? he wondered.) "You are a delightful young lady, and your cheerful mood is infectious." Sounds like a testimonial. "But in a work environment such as this a greater degree of dignity and decorum would be more in place."

"You mean I'm too bouncy, Doctor Wainright?"

"Bouncy is certainly one of the adjectives which come to mind," Charlie allowed. "And while we're on the subject of bouncing, we really must do something about our nipples."

"We, Doctor Wainright?" The conversation was taking a surprising turn.

"A slip of the tongue," he said, unconsciously moistening his lips. "But I think you must agree, Miss Saunders, that they are a trifle—er—provocative."

"I'm awfully sorry, Doctor Wainright," Miss Saunders said demurely. "I didn't realize they provoked you."

"I didn't say they provoked me," he quibbled.

"Well, they certainly don't provoke me. If they're provocative they must be provoking somebody, and I'd like to know who."

"Does it really matter whom they provoke, Miss Saunders?" (This woman really is most provoking, thought Charlie.) "So long as we agree they must provoke somebody."

"Certainly it matters. A girl has a right to know who her nipples are provoking."

"Whom," he corrected involuntarily. "Whom they are provoking. Anyway, how would you propose to find out? Place an ad in the newspaper?"

"How else could you find out? How would you word it? Do nipples provoke you? Do Miss Saunders' nipples provoke you? Are you provoked by nipples? Are Miss . . ."

"Possibly," he interrupted hastily, "and I hesitate to mention such a personal matter, possibly if you were to wear a brassiere that might help."

"Oh but I do!" she assured him. "I wouldn't dare go without." She breathed in deeply. "See what I mean?"

"Be careful!" Charlie yelped. "That's positively dangerous. You don't know what could happen."

"Oh but I do," she assured him again. "They've got out of control before. I always wear a bra."

Charlie gazed enthralled. "~~Unbelievable~~," ~~he murmured~~.

"Well, really!" She was incensed. "If you don't believe me I can prove it. Here."

The pink sweater could not have been very securely anchored by the wide black belt. Miss Saunders crossed her arms, took hold of the sweater at each side and drew it up over her head. "Now do you believe me?"

He had to believe her. Her bust was certainly enclosed, but only just, the nipples straining through the flimsy covering. Like cherries on a dish of jello, he thought. "I apologize, Miss Saunders," he said, breathing hard. "I really didn't doubt the truth of your statement."

"I should hope not. How would it sound in court? 'Well, your honor, I had to take my clothes off in front of my boss just to prove I was telling the truth.' I should have to tell the whole truth, so help me."

"Make a clean breast of it?" Charlie suggested.

"I shall treat that comment with ignore, Doctor Wainright."

"I'm sorry. This whole thing seems to be getting quite unreal."

"Doctor Wainright!" Miss Saunders stamped her foot, setting up vibrations that threatened the integrity of the restraining structure. "Of course they're real! How can you doubt it?"

She can't be serious, thought Charlie. She'd never go that far. Maybe she would, though. One can but try.

"They certainly do stretch the credulity," he said, more in hope than expectation.

"There you go again. You don't want to believe anything I say. I guess I've got to prove it again."

The brassiere unhooked at the front. In an instant she had it in her hand, and flung it onto the desk. "There. How much further do I have to go to get some respect?"

Charlie swallowed hard. "Don't for god's sake go any further than this room dressed like that," he pleaded. "Anyway, I think this is about all I can handle for now."

"I wouldn't dream of letting you handle them, Doctor Wainright!" She stamped the other foot, and set the whole apparatus quivering like a seismograph in a force eight earthquake. Charlie restrained himself with difficulty from reaching out to damp the vibrations.

"We . . ." He was interrupted by the beep of the telephone. His hand reached for the instrument while his eyes stayed mesmerized by the phenomenon before him.

"Wainright," he said into the phone.

"Topham here, Sir." Miss Saunders could hear the fruity foghorn quite clearly. "Miss Gwynn has arrived, Sir. She says she's a bit early."

"Ohmygawd, you can say that again, Topham." Charlie looked up frantically at the twin portents of a shattered career. "Stall her, Topham, will you?"

"Sorry Sir, she's already on her way up."

Charlie slammed down the telephone. "Miss Gwynn," he hissed. "Beat it, quick."

But Miss Saunders was two jiggles ahead of him. She had already gathered up her sweater and was halfway to the door.

Even in this extreme emergency, time stood still while Charlie gazed fascinated at the complex gyrations of human machinery on the run, and pondered on the way an attraction out of control could become a sensation.

A sharp rap on the outer door snapped him back to real time. The lock gate opened and Miss Gwynn sailed in, full rigged and all flags flying.

Hurrah for the Constitution, he thought. Thank god we're both on the same side. So far.

"I'm early," the Chairman of the Board announced unnecessarily as Charlie rose to greet her. She came majestically alongside and berthed in the chair opposite. "But I'm sure you don't mind, do you, Doctor Wainright?"

Ship of the line, twenty-seven guns, practically unsinkable, Charlie decided. Five feet ten from water line to topmast, and what a prow! She could have been a showgirl fifteen years ago with a superstructure like that. And speaking of superstructure, Miss Saunders had better get that sweater on double quick or we'll both be sunk without trace.

"No problem, Miss Gwynn," he assured her. "Just glad you could come."

"Mizz," said Miss Gwynn.

"I beg you pardon?"

"Mizz," repeated Miss Gwynn. "I'm very particular about titles and forms of address, you know. You wouldn't like me to call you Mister now, would you, Doctor Wainright?"

"I do see your point," he said apologetically. Bad choice of words there. Better get the mind off anatomical details and think about the budget. He reached for the folder on his desk. And froze! Draped across it was a small heap of material, lace trimmed and trailing various shoulder straps and elastic.

The sharp eyes of the look-out aboard the Constitution had evidently noticed at the same moment.

"What is that, Doctor Wainright?" Miss Gwynn's voice had taken on the feminine silkiness that usually accompanied her defenseless-female-in-a-rough-man's-world mode. Better grab the bull by the horns, thought Charlie, aware that the figure of speech was far from appropriate. He lifted the file carefully and tilted it, allowing the item to cascade to the desk.

"About thirty-six D, I would think," he estimated.

"Brassiere, you know. Lady's brassiere. Not, of course, that there's any other kind of brassiere. Unless you put one on a cow, but that's anudder matter altogether."

"I don't want you to think me overly inquisitive, Doctor Wainright." This time it was the I'm-a-woman-and-proud-of-it voice. "But isn't it just a teeny bit strange for you to be keeping a brassiere on your desk?"

"A very natural question, Miss Gwynn—er, Mizz Gwynn." Charlie was thinking fast. If he could dodge those broadsides he might be able to get out of range. "In fact, Mizz Gwynn, my secretary was remarking the same thing only ten minutes ago. She said, if I remember correctly, 'You don't hardly find many brassieres on administrators' desks these days.' And she was right, you know. You don't. Thing of the past nowadays, really, when you come to think about it. But we don't want to take up the time of the Chairman of the Board talking about brassieres, do we? You came here to talk about the budget."

But Miss Gwynn had the wind astern and was not about to alter course or give up the chase. "You've piqued my curiosity now, Doctor Wainright. You must have a very good reason for keeping that—er—that, on your desk." This time it was the hortatory mode, brooking no refusal.

"Mizz Gwynn." Charlie lowered his voice and looked guiltily at the door. "I'm going to have to let you into a little secret now that you've caught me in flagrante delicto, so to speak." How nearly right that was! "I didn't want anyone to know about it just yet, but after all you are different, are you not? For some time now it has seemed to me all wrong that we should have a Museum of Man and no Museum of Woman. So I was toying with the idea of a section devoted to things we consider to be in Woman's domain.

Childbirth, for instance. That marvelous feminine thing called intuition. Cosmetics. Cookery . . ."

"Not cookery, Doctor Wainright." Nearly slipped up there.

"No, certainly not cookery. Of course not. And then there are brassieres. So entirely feminine, don't you think? I mean, you don't see men wearing brassieres. Not that you really see women wearing them, of course. More's the pity. I thought we could have a display of the brassieres of the women leaders of our age. Rather along the lines of gloves of famous boxers, you know."

"And this is to be an exhibit? Rather a flimsy one, isn't it?" The anything-you-can-do-I-can-do-better light was in her eye. "Who does it belong to, may I ask?"

"I really don't think it would be discreet to reveal names at this juncture, Mizz Gwynn. Let me just say that this lady is being exceptionally cooperative. I only wish there were more like her." Charlie turned on a smile whose charm and persuasiveness Lawton would have considered sickening. "I was wondering how I was going to broach the subject to you yourself. As one of the leaders of this community you will certainly wish to contribute to the exhibit?"

"Really, Doctor Wainright, I don't know what to say."

This time it was pure how-nice-of-you-to-think-of-little-me.

"This subject is just a wee bit—er—intimate for a lady to be discussing with a gentleman, isn't it? At least, during office hours."

"Mizz Gwynn, I'm sure it can do no harm for you to be intimate with me," Charlie assured her. "That is to say, to discuss it with me even though you may be concerned about its intimate connotations. I see your brassiere, Mizz Gwynn, figuratively speaking, of course, as the cornerstone, the centerpiece, the main attraction of our exhibit. In fact, as I look at you now," he was going to regret this, but he couldn't stop now, "I see a life size plaster cast of the bust of Rosemary Gwynn facing us as we enter the door of the Museum of Woman, with a recording of the massed pipes of the Fifty Fourth Highland Regiment playing tastefully in the background. How does that grab you, Miss G?"

"You flatter me, Doctor Wainright." She was almost twittering. "But I could never be party to such a thing."

"Sure you could," Charlie insisted. "All you have to do is Gwynn and bare it."

CHAPTER 9

At the studios of WFUN-TV, Michael Flynn, like many an interviewer before him, had always found the Chesney personality a natural for the talk show format.

Lawton Wainright anticipated no difficulty with the routine. After the usual puff for Chesney's act at the Tight Owl, Lawton began to answer, reasonably enough, questions about his early life and career. Reasonably enough for a Chesney interview, at least. Chesney made a point of never giving the same version twice. This time he had been born in Outer Mongolia, the sixth child of a poor Scottish shepherd and a Hungarian Gypsy girl.

"I suppose I'm sticking my neck out," Flynn ventured, knowing perfectly well that he was. He was no novice at interviewing comedians. "But I'll risk it. Why would a Scottish shepherd and a Hungarian Gypsy girl be in Outer Mongolia?"

"No problem." Lawton smiled innocently. "At that time Father was on an archaeological dig in the ruins of the lost capital of Bazookistan. Mother thought it would be nice to have a Mongolian in the family. She'd never had a Mongolian baby before, you see. She'd had Mongolian barbecue, but that wasn't the same thing at all. Not nearly so filling. Willy was born in Peru, Angus was Indian, Charlene was Armenian, Farouk was Egyptian, and Lin Hwong Chow was Scottish. By the time she had me she'd found out what was causing all the pregnancies, so I was the last. The Gypsies used to have some sort of idea the music was responsible, but it wasn't really, you know."

"Wait a minute." Flynn never liked his guests to hog the camera. That was his prerogative. The Flynn Show was designed to keep Flynn in front of the camera. The guests were there to attract the viewers. "Let's just get this straight. Your parents had children in Peru and India and Armenia and . . ."

"And Egypt. And Scotland, of course." Lawton had the ball again, and ran with it. "That was rather a mistake, actually. They were going out to China, and they left it a bit late. Mother was pregnant with Lin Hwong Chow, and just before the boat sailed she went into labour. That's mother, not Lin Hwong Chow. So she had to stay behind in Scotland.

She didn't mind, really. She'd never liked Chinese food. Gypsies don't you know."

"I thought you said she liked Mongolian food." Flynn had caught him out.

"No, I said she'd had Mongolian barbecue. I didn't say she liked it. She didn't like me very much, either. Besides, Mongolian food and Chinese food aren't the same thing at all. Now, (don't stop me now, Michael!) I expect you're wondering why Father, who was a Scottish shepherd, would be digging around in the ruins of ancient civilizations. You're not the first to wonder about that. I wondered about it myself, as a matter of fact."

Charlie could churn out this sort of nonsense without even thinking about it. It flowed out of Lawton, and Lawton found himself enjoying it.

"The problem was, Mother couldn't stand the smell of sheep. I know Gypsies are supposed to eat a lot of mutton, but that's why Mother gave up the Gypsy business. Couldn't stand the smell. Of the mutton, not the Gypsies. So she made Mcgregor give up shepherding and sent him to college. Went around telling fortunes and getting her palm crossed with paper money and made enough to pay his way. Actually, she thought he was going to be a high priced corporate lawyer, but it turned out he'd signed up for the wrong course and he came out an archaeologist. That's why they traveled about so much, you see. Funny how things work out, isn't it? If Mother hadn't puked at the smell of sheep I wouldn't be Mongolian. Outer Mongolian, that is. And if McGregor hadn't been a Scot I might never have taught myself to play the bagpipes."

Someone squatting down beside one of the cameras was giving Flynn the signal to cut away for the commercial.

"That sounds like the perfect music cue," Flynn cut Lawton short. "I happen to know that you've brought along your bagpipes, so we'll come back to you for a tune right after this message."

During the commercial Lawton's mind turned to Linda. She had come with him to the studio and was sitting somewhere on the blind side of the lights. Good kid. Getting a bit protective, though. More than just a gleam of marriage in the eye, too. Been acting rather strangely today. Said something about not talking about this morning, but there hadn't been time to pursue it further.

After the commercial, Lawton was at the piano playing idly with the keys, his pipes out of their case on the stool beside him. He looked out at the audience, and pretended to pick his nose. When he resumed playing, the finger stuck to the keys. Once this was sorted out he looked back over his shoulder at Flynn.

"This is one of my routines. Instant song writing. Give me a tune and I'll put words to it. Or give me words and I'll put them to music. Take your pick. Which will you have?"

"I can't think of any words right now," Flynn said. Why can't the sonofabitch tell me what he's going to do? Just trying to get one up on me, the asshole. "Do you want me to give you the name of a song, or do I have to hum the tune?"

"For god's sake don't hum. Just the name will do."

"Alright, how about White Christmas?"

"No problem." He started to play the melody. "Now, what do you want me to sing about? Snow?"

"Certainly not snow. Nor Christmas."

"The moon? Love?"

"Gypsies!" yelled someone in the audience, and raised a laugh. Flynn picked it up immediately.

"There you go, Charlie. A request from the studio audience. Let's see what you can do with gypsies and White Christmas."

Lawton made a face into the camera. "Gypsies? You're kidding. Alright, if that's what you want."

He played on quietly to the end of the verse, thinking. Then, looking into the camera, he began.

"I'm dreaming of a white gypsy,
Just like my mother used to be.
I've a secret sorrow,
When I wake tomorrow
I shan't know who I'm s'posed to be.

Miss Saunders' bust is fantastic,
Miss Gwynn's could sink a battleship.
Now Miss Gwynn's a real sexy broad,
But she's also the Chairman of the Board."

Lawton stopped, and got up from the piano. "That's quite enough of that."

"I quite agree," Michael Flynn said humorlessly. "What did it mean?"

"I haven't the least idea," Lawton admitted.

"But who's Miss Saunders, and who's Miss Gwynn?"

"Haven't the foggiest notion, Michael. Just seemed to come into my head. Seemed to make sense at the time. Didn't you like it? Well, here's an altogether different experience. You'll love this."

He picked up the bagpipes, made a great play of arranging them under his arm, blew into them to fill the bag, and then held the chanter away in disgust at the discordant squeal that filled the studio.

"You have to be kind to them," he explained. "If you don't treat them well they won't do a thing for you. But before you learn to play the pipes you have to know the names of all the parts. For instance, this bit is called the—er—anyone remember what this bit is called?"

There followed some by-play with the audience, punctuated by squawks from the pipes seemingly without cause, at which

Lawton feigned surprise. "Now this one's easy. This bag shaped thing is called, with that frankness for which the Scots are justly famed, The Bag. People will tell you the bag is made from the stomach of a sheep. Don't you believe it. Not true. Can you imagine what a sheep's stomach would smell like? After it's been dead a few years? Even alive it's bad enough. My mother could never bear to be in the same room with a sheep, with or without its stomach. No, the bag is made from genooine haggis skin. After the edible parts of the haggis have been eaten, of course. The haggis has to be just the right age. Too young and it's not big enough, too old and it's too tough and inflexible. About four years old is the best age, and coincidentally that happens to be the best age for eating them. Haggis not bagpipes. You can't eat bagpipes."

Throughout this monologue Lawton had been pausing to blow into the mouthpiece, punching and squeezing the bag, and producing a variety of wails and shrieks. Finally, he gave up in disgust, and flung the pipes back down onto the piano stool. While the audience applauded he went back to the couch and confronted Michael Flynn.

Flynn was obviously nonplussed. "I thought you were going to play them?"

"I just did. Where were you? Didn't you listen?"

"But—that's not all you do with them, surely?"

"Michael," Lawton said severely, "it's all I do with them in front of a family audience. What else do you suggest I do, if it's not a rude answer?"

"I thought you were going to play something properly." Flynn was prepared to be offensive. "You do play them, don't you?"

"Well, I thought that was pretty good myself. For a Mongolian. How about you?" Lawton appealed to the audience, making faces and nodding his head at Flynn and going through the motions of clapping his hands. The audience responded with prolonged applause and whistles while he stood to take a bow. When all was quiet again he stood leaning on Flynn's desk, looking down at him.

"The trouble with you is, you expect the Argyle and Sutherland Highlanders. You wouldn't get their mascot for the paltry twenty five bucks you're paying me. However, I'll have another go if you insist. You do insist, I suppose?"

"Certainly," Flynn said. "If you're any good I'll make it another five bucks." He was astute enough to latch onto the momentum of the laughter.

Lawton waved to the audience and stomped back to his pipes. "I'll have a try at something I wrote myself," he told them, deliberately ignoring Flynn. "It's called 'McDougal McNab and McKay, or the Lament of the Lost Haggis.' It's a very sad piece."

It was a rousing, intricate piece, and he played it well, marching and counter-marching, dancing, clowning, pretending to be running out of breath and holding the pipes at arms' length while they continued to produce music. The audience loved it. After the applause, he went back to the couch again.

Flynn was laughing. "You really had me fooled. I wasn't sure you really could play the things."

"You should hear me in my kilt," Lawton said, leaping up to begin a Highland Fling. "The pipes always sound better in a kilt. When I'm in a kilt, that is. You know what I mean."

The next guest was an English historian on tour, drumming up publicity for his most recent book. Doctor Gerald Moore, in his early fifties, balding, bespectacled, strode across the stage with a bouncing step. He was a foremost authority on Middle Eastern culture, and Flynn was not at all sure how well this interview would follow the virtual variety show just concluded. Particularly since Moore's favorite line seemed to be, "Please don't comment on my English accent. As far as I'm concerned you have the accent, not me." And he had already worked that to death before the show.

Lawton moved along the couch to make room for him as they were introduced. "I've already read 'Egypt, Cradle of Culture,' Doctor Moore," he said, shaking his hand. "I was particularly impressed with your analysis of the contribution of the Fifteenth Dynasty.

Few historians seem to have grasped the immense significance of that period to cultural advancement throughout the world. Mainly, I suppose, owing to the dearth of written records from that period."

The interview was not going according to plan. Flynn's plan. He lifted up the book that had been lying on his desk beside the microphone and held it toward one of the cameras, moving it from side to side to attract the director's attention. The red light above the camera lit and, uncharacteristically, Flynn looked straight into the lens. He usually found the blank, unresponsive cyclops unnerving. Informal chat was easier than direct discourse, his inevitable flubs less noticeable, if not a part of the Talk Show technique. But Cheerful Charlie Chesney was getting altogether too much attention.

"I always make a point of reading the books that come across my desk," he began, "but I must confess . . ."

"Thank you Mr. Chesney," Dr. Moore said. He had turned toward Lawton in some surprise. "Isn't this rather an unusual interest for a comedian?"

Flynn tried again. "Doctor Moore has succeeded in making what might seem a rather obscure subject come to life for the . . ."

"We're not all morons." Lawton was unconscious of the interruption, so involved in his favorite subject. "We all have our little interests. Fifteenth Dynasty Egypt happens to be one of mine. I was interested in your conclusion that the two-horse chariot was the greatest invention of the era, but you know I just can't agree with you at all."

Flynn was really annoyed. Interviews were designed for interviewers, not for celebrities. But if he couldn't stop the discussion, he could at least insert himself into the key position again. "Why don't you tell us what was so special about the chariot, Doctor Moore?" he interjected desperately, fearful of being beached by a receding tide of technicality.

"Not just the chariot," Lawton corrected him sharply. "The two-horse chariot. The one-horse chariot was already in existence."

Moore was fired up by the criticism. "But my dear chap, don't you see that double-harnessing opened up the way for the deployment of more power in every kind of vehicle? Wagons could carry more produce, two oxen to a plough made cultivation of larger areas possible, and so on."

"No doubt about that, no doubt at all," agreed Lawton.

"I really don't think . . ." Flynn began.

"Very far-reaching influence indeed," agreed Lawton.

"It doesn't seem to me . . ." said Flynn.

"But my own contention is," Lawton went on, "that it was the development of the upright loom that was far more influential on the whole way of life of the civilized world at that time. Overnight almost, textiles changed from crude, loosely woven, single-color, poor quality material. There was an explosion of color, of design, of style. Think of the effect on the entire cultural development of the Middle East. The woven product became superior, sought after by other countries. Export trade from Ancient Egypt increased incredibly. International commerce blossomed, peace treaties were made, frontiers opened up."

But no one was listening, other than Doctor Moore. Flynn had signaled the director to kill the two microphones that Lawton and Moore wore round their necks, and was already introducing the next guest.

Valerie Fuchs, diminutive, fortyish, dressed in khaki shirt and shorts and tropical sun helmet, made her entrance like a circus performer, stepping quickly from behind the curtain and running lightly across the stage holding a chain in each outstretched hand. At the end of each chain shambled a cheerful chimpanzee, evidently happy for the activity after the long back-stage wait.

Valerie Fuchs was the latest in the succession of female anthropologists returning from Darkest Africa after a stint living among the apes. The interview was not destined to enlighten viewers on the activities of anthropologists in Africa, but it would became famous as the first item in an altogether novel style of Talk Show, one that would come to be known as the Flynn Flamm.

Flynn had just risen to greet the lady, deliberately ignoring his first two guests and applauding with the audience as Miss Fuchs swept across the stage, arms raised high and apes deployed on either side. It was not the lady's fault that a triumphal progress was dramatically transformed into a dramatic tableau. It was Maurice who was to blame. Maurice, the larger of her two companions, quite simply decided to stop dead in his tracks and leer at the studio audience. Miss Fuchs, with the chain wrapped securely round her left wrist, was instantly jerked to a halt in mid-stride with her left arm outstretched.

Maureen, attached to the other wrist, reached the end of the slack in her chain and also came to a sudden stop.

Miss Fuchs' other arm shot out at right angles from her body, her whole frame seemed to lift into the air, and in an instant she was flat on her back on the stage.

The image of a spread-eagled female apparently having her arms torn out of their sockets by chained wild animals like a Christian in the Roman arena was not lost on the camera operators, who zoomed in appreciatively for close-ups. But it was Maurice who stole the scene. With a look of simian delight, he grinned out at the audience, gently rocking from one foot to the other and urinating copiously on the carpet.

Flynn was delighted. The show so far had given every indication of being a catastrophe because of his own inability to control the interviews. But suddenly it was taking off. He waited, content to leave the director and camera crew between them to milk the situation for every possible laugh. Ideas were already taking shape in his mind. First was the thought that here was a way to get even with those horses' asses on the couch and make them look foolish. Then came the realization that there were program possibilities, and a sure-fire way to salvage even the slowest interview. And finally came the brain wave. A whole new talk show format built on unexpected situations that made people laugh at the guests. So celebrities didn't go for being laughed at? They were so hungry for publicity they'd do anything. They'd be lining up for the chance to be on the Flynn Show. And they would know exactly what to expect. The unexpected!

Lawton and Moore moved along the couch to make way for Miss Fuchs. Flynn went through the formality of introducing them, insisted that they move far enough to make room for the two chimpanzees on the couch, but otherwise ignored them.

"Does he do that often?" he asked when they were all settled.

"Who?" Miss Fuchs looked round at Doctor Moore. "Oh, Maurice. Well, he's just like you, you know. What goes in must come out. So I guess he does it about five times a day." She seemed rather surprised by the question.

"On the carpet, I mean," Flynn corrected.

"Only when he wants to show off. Or when he can't wait. Usually we time it better than this, but one of your people backstage gave him a can of coke."

Maurice was already bored, and turned his attention to the interesting hairless human beside him. Clambering to the back of the couch, he energetically picked through the sparse locks on either side of Moore's head, then bent his head and planted a long kiss on the shining scalp.

"Oh, I'm so sorry," Miss Fuchs apologized with some embarrassment, as she became aware of Dr. Moore attempting to disengage.

"I'm sure Doctor Moore loves the attention he's getting," Flynn said maliciously. "Let Maurice enjoy himself. I didn't know chimps liked Coke."

"Maurice does." Miss Fuchs made sure the two chains were securely round her right wrist and turned back to Flynn. "Maureen doesn't though. She won't touch it. She's a Pepsi girl."

Maureen, hearing her name, decided there was no way she was going to sit quietly while Maurice was allowed to enjoy himself. Climbing across Moore's knees, she landed on Lawton's lap, where she lay back and looked adoringly up into his face. Maurice, having exhausted the potential of a bald head, climbed down between the two men, looping his chain round Moore's neck, and leaped back across the Doctor's lap to rejoin his owner. The momentum of the leap tightened the chain on Miss Fuchs' wrist. Miss Fuchs' right arm once more shot out sideways, this time behind Doctor Moore's neck. The chain round Doctor Moore's neck jerked his head abruptly towards Miss Fuchs. Miss Fuchs fell abruptly against Doctor Moore, and put out her other arm to cling convulsively round his neck.

Maurice climbed quietly onto the back of the couch and tightened the chain.

Maureen, seeing the two humans apparently amorously entwined, was evidently aroused to similar desires. Seductively, she reached up to put her arms round Lawton's neck, pulled herself up to his level, and pressed her nose to his while she gazed into his eyes.

It was at that moment Lawton felt the giddiness. It was as if the seat beneath him had dropped away and he was falling into space. He closed his eyes against both the vertigo and the appalling proximity of the chimpanzee's face and breath. And then, with incredible and absolute clearness, he heard the voice of his secretary, Miss Saunders.

"For a stuffy old archaeologist you certainly seem to have a fixation on nipples," said the voice. And he heard himself reply, though he could never have believed that such words could have come from him, "Anyone'd be happy to get a fix on those babies."

He opened his eyes, but his whole field of vision was filled by the out-of-focus hairiness of Maureen's face an inch from his. Still falling, still listening like an eavesdropper to the conversation with his secretary, he reached up frantically to disengage the chimpanzee's arms from his neck. Maureen responded by smacking her lips wetly and noisily, then clamping her mouth firmly to his in a stifling kiss. He closed his eyes and tried to scream, struggling harder with the arms round his neck. But the scream was stifled and the arms only clung the tighter. And the falling grew faster.

Then, just as in a thousand falling dreams, it was over. A sensation of relief surged through him. The arms relaxed their hold and he was able to remove them. The mouth released his and he was able to breathe. He opened his eyes and looked into the startled eyes of Miss Saunders.

CHAPTER 10

Three of the four participants in the latest Change became aware of it with vastly different emotions. (It is doubtful if the fourth was aware of much more than a desire for attention and the limitation of her chain.)

For Lawton Wainright, there was an overwhelming sense of escape, together with an almost clinical awareness that The Change had now evolved from a waking-in-the-morning phenomenon to a might-happen-any-time event. Only as an afterthought did it occur to him that of all the predicaments he could have been dropped into there were far worse fates than being attacked by a sexy secretary.

Charlie Chesney, on the other hand, had experienced nothing in his past that would prepare him at a moment's notice to resist the advances of a love-struck chimpanzee.

Charlie might have been vaguely aware that there had developed something new in the pattern of The Change, but with an amorous ape one inch away from his face, drawing in her breath for a further oscillatory exercise, very little else was registering in his mind.

Miss Saunders, alone of the three, knew exactly where she was and what she was doing. But even she found the developing situation incomprehensible. It was quite outside her experience that a red-blooded, presumably healthy male, who had spent the past five minutes encouraging her indiscretion, should suddenly exhibit every sign of panic and behave like a professional virgin in a whorehouse. Hence the startled look that was the first detail to meet Lawton's eyes on arrival.

It was some moments before Lawton could gather his wits enough to realize that he was in his office at the museum, with a far sexier mammal than Maureen on his lap. Her face was now a little further from his than Maureen's had been, and he still had her hands in his after pulling her arms from around his neck. He dropped her hands and put his own to his face. "Whoo! What a relief!" he gasped.

"Well, really!" Miss Saunders said indignantly. "That's not very nice! You sound as if you've escaped a fate worse than death."

"I have. You can't imagine how awful it was."

"I certainly can't. My shorthand may not be up to much, Doctor Wainright, but I've never had any complaints about my smooching. I've never been so insulted. Almost never."

"I didn't mean it that way at all, Miss Saunders," Lawton stammered. "Really, I'm dreadfully sorry."

"So am I. I'm so embarrassed. You shouldn't encourage a girl like that. Anyway, what was wrong with it?"

He looked at her wide eyes, at the mouth that Charlie had evidently been encouraging, and lowered his eyes in embarrassment. What his eyes encountered next sent the blood rushing to his face in a blush that reached to the tips of his ears. So that was the reason for the conversation he had overheard just before The Change. A fixation on nipples, she had said. Hastily he looked away, up again into her face, dared not meet her eyes, and looked wildly over her shoulder and out into the room. Anywhere but at that unbuttoned blouse, those creamy globes and those aggressively naked nipples.

"I don't know how to explain it, Miss Nipples—Miss Saunders." He was beginning to babble. He had to explain somehow. But how? "You just can't think how horrible it is to be kissed by a female chimpanzee."

"You rotten beast! What a lousy thing to say!" Miss Saunders slid off his lap and stood in front of him, her eyes brimming with tears. "It's all been fun up till now but that's a filthy thing to say."

"Miss Saunders, I really didn't mean anything like that at all." The embarrassment was gone in an instant as he saw that she was really hurt. She wants to cry but she's determined not to, he thought.

Nice girl, she's not just turning on the tears for effect. He hated himself for hurting her, for not being more careful what he said. But how could he explain?

He jumped to his feet to comfort her, miserably aware of how difficult it was for him to show emotion. He wanted to put his arms round her, let her cry if she needed to, explain what he had meant to say, but he was too shy to approach her. Particularly with her blouse wide open. In the office. If only she would cover those—Things! But as she stood with her head up, sniffing and defiantly trying to maintain her dignity, the Things only seemed to catch her mood and stand up as defiantly themselves. In his mind he struggled with excuses, explanations, something that could be remotely believable. But nothing came to him. Instead, an elusive, aching yearning drove out all other thoughts. And then the memory of Linda was there. Linda, so warm and loving and full of tenderness when he desperately needed help. And immediately the shyness was gone, and he knew that all he had to do was what Linda would have done. He heard himself say, "Don't be hurt, Baby. Come to me. Come to me and let me tell you what happened."

She went to him, and he found his arms going about her quite naturally, almost as if she were a child, yet he had never felt at ease with children. He held her close to him, and kissed her wet eyes. And when she had relaxed in his arms, he bent his head lower and gently kissed her mouth. There was no love in it, no sex, but it gave the message that healed the earlier hurt.

She looked up at him and smiled wryly. "Not really so bad, was it?"

It was to Linda that he felt unfaithful, not to Claire. But it was as if Linda had said, "You've hurt her, go ahead and kiss it better. I shan't mind."

He kissed her again then, and it was Linda in his arms. Linda, who was lost to him on the other side unless he could get back to her again. Linda, who seemed to fill his thoughts as if she were part of his real life. At last, they drew apart and looked at each other, smiling. Lawton wondered momentarily whether the office door was locked, and what would happen if Miss Gwynn should walk in on them. And surprised himself by deciding it was of no importance. More like the way Chesney would behave, he thought. He looked down at Miss Saunders' open blouse, and found himself doing up the buttons for her with no slightest feeling of embarrassment. There was a self-confidence in him that he had never felt before, a bravado almost. He knew there must be a part of Charlie Chesney still remaining with him.

There was another difference that he was becoming conscious of. Before, when he had wakened in the morning to find himself back in his own home, remembrance of the other experience had quickly faded. This time the memories were still there. So was an awareness of all that had happened during the time Chesney had been in his place, though those memories were in a different compartment from his own. As if they belonged to someone else. But which were his own memories? Lawton Wainright had apparently locked his wife in the bathroom and encouraged Miss Saunders to take off her clothes and behaved generally quite irresponsibly, and yet Lawton was feeling no responsibility for all of that. Only concern about how it was all to be sorted out. Charlie Chesney had apparently made love to Linda McClusky and antagonized Michael Flynn and forfeited any chance of a return appearance on the Flynn Show, and yet it was Lawton Wainright who claimed those memories as his own. If the situation had been upsetting before, it was going to be chaotic now, with an awareness of two separate lives in his mind.

There still remained the problem of how to explain to Miss Saunders. He obviously could never tell her what had really happened. She would think he was out of his mind. Only Linda could understand. And possibly Jeff, but he was not too sure even about Jeff. He would have to dream up some story that she could accept, though it was against his nature to lie to her.

"That chimpanzee business," he said. "It was some sort of hallucination. I've been having a lot of them lately."

"I don't think I understand," Miss Saunders said stiffly.

"I don't know how you could understand if you haven't experienced it," he said. This part was true, anyway. "It's a feeling that I'm suddenly somewhere else, sometimes even somebody else altogether. It's a horrible feeling, you can't imagine how terrifying it is, the panic just floods over you." Pile it on thick, play on her sympathy, he thought cynically, blaming Chesney's influence yet resenting the intrusion into his private thoughts.

"It sounds awful." Miss Saunders' sympathy was aroused. "But where does the chimpanzee come in?"

"This time I suddenly seemed to find myself sitting on a couch with this chimp named Maureen climbing all over me. It all seemed so real."

"And you thought it was the chimp kissing you? How absolutely vile! And I was so horrid to you. I'm so sorry, I should have known you wouldn't try to be beastly."

Lawton took out his handkerchief and dabbed at one of her eyes where a tear still lingered. "It's I who should apologize, Miss Saunders. You shouldn't have to be concerned with my problems. This might never have happened if Jeff Sangster hadn't cancelled this afternoon's high school tour, so why don't we blame him?"

She stood irresolute for a moment as he walked across to see whether the door had been locked. There was more to be said from her point of view.

"I realize it must be pretty rotten for you when these things come on," she said. "I'd like to be able to help you, if you'll let me. But right now I've got a problem too. Five minutes ago you were Joe Octopus. I couldn't have fought you off even if I'd wanted to. And I didn't. Now I'm suddenly Miss Saunders again and you're the boss. I feel kind of stupid."

He wanted to take her in his arms again. He tried to blame Chesney for it, but he could feel that Linda had awakened instincts he had long suppressed as ungentlemanly in a married man. Anyway, did he really owe any loyalty to Claire? But this was, after all, a business office, and there could only be one code of conduct in the office.

"Miss Saunders," he said, wishing he could be proper without sounding so prim, "I have behaved outrageously. Whatever my personal and masculine feelings towards you there can be no excuse for such behavior in the office. I'm sure your respect for me cannot but be enhanced by a degree of self-control on my part."

But she started it all! She was the one flaunting her nipples in the first place! And the second place. She likes taking off her clothes, so why not keep her happy? A happy staff is an efficient staff, isn't that the way it goes? Chesney was still there interfering in his thoughts. Such intrusion was intolerable! Didn't the man have any sense of office decorum? All right, so the office is so damn sacred, but here's a chick with big boobs and her pants on fire and the right kind of ambition, so don't waste it. There's other times and other places if you don't want it in the office. Besides, Chesney will return, you can bet on that, so don't louse it up for Chesney, eh?

Keep out; keep out of my life, Lawton thought. You're killing my self-respect, and you could lose me my job as well. But aloud he said, "Why don't we take up where we left off after office hours? Then I can behave outrageously without feeling so guilty about it." Not what he had meant to say, but it seemed to have satisfied Chesney, because there was no further intrusion.

It was not till he was driving home that he really had time to indulge himself and let his mind review the day's activities since his escape from Maureen. First, there had been all the correspondence that Chesney had neglected. Then he had had to review his notes for the Elgin lecture. And finally there had been the lecture itself, gratifyingly well received, all things considered. Thank god he'd come back in time to deliver it himself! He shuddered to think what Chesney could have done to the occasion. Or supposing The Change had occurred right in the middle of the lecture? There seemed to be no reason to expect them to happen at convenient times any more. The last time had been convenient enough, certainly. But only for him. Chesney had presumably dropped right into the middle of a clinch with Maureen.

In the first minutes after he found himself in the office with Miss Saunders, the problem of picking up the pieces of his own life where Chesney had left them occupied all his attention. It had not entered his head that there might be more Changes to come, almost certainly would be. Now that he had time to think about it, his first thought was that he would be able to see Linda again, might be seeing her, on and off, for a long time to come. Then came the realization that his life and his career could continue to be disrupted by Chesney's insane behavior, on and off, for an equally long time to come. But was it only his life that was being disrupted? He, after all, was doing his best to alienate Chesney's girl, and he had made a good job of ruining the television appearance. What on earth might he do if he actually had to do Chesney's act at the Tight Owl?

Up till today they only seemed to have been influencing each other while they were actually in each others' places. But now, even in his own life, he was constantly aware of Chesney's thoughts affecting his own. It was only a matter of time before Chesney would be influencing his behavior, and life would be a constant tug-of-war between them. Perhaps Chesney was experiencing the same problem? Were his thoughts intruding into Chesney's life? Not consciously, certainly, or intentionally, but there was no reason to suppose he was not. They always said only ten percent of the human brain was actually in use. Presumably he and Chesney were using some of the other ninety percent?

Chesney had made him leave the door open to the possibility of a continuing liaison with Miss Saunders. Was he at the same time persuading Chesney to put in a word for him with Linda? He could feel no guilt if this were the case, because Linda was just another cute chick to Chesney. Linda! He was becoming obsessed with her. Obsessed with a girl who only existed in a fantasy world! And yet Charlie Chesney was no fantasy, he was there every night at the Tight Owl. So did Linda also really exist? Could he go to the Tight Owl tonight and find Linda watching Chesney's act? Could he meet her there? Would she know him? Of course not, she had never seen how he really looked. Would she want to know him, or was his Linda a different Linda in a parallel universe who only existed during The Change?

When would it happen again? It could be at any moment, apparently, not just while he was asleep. Was there any point in planning anything more in this life, if Chesney was likely to arrive at any time and do whatever he wanted with it? This thing was becoming an obsession. And why not? It was not so much the trauma of The Change itself now as the threat of Chesney's asinine behavior. And the prospect of seeing Linda again. He was going to have to keep a tight grip on himself or this thing could send him round the bend. Perhaps he was already round the bend? Perhaps that was what all this was about? Perhaps he should see a psychiatrist. Perhaps he should go and see Chesney and find out whether all this was really happening to him.

But what if Chesney only laughed at him? And Linda too. Did he really want to know whether she was real or not?

CHAPTER 11

Charlie Chesney mixed himself a gin and tonic, and threw himself down in front of the television. He was not in a good mood.

"Why did you have to take him there in the first place?" he yelled through the open door. "You might have known the horse's ass would cock up the whole damn thing."

Linda McClusky came out of the bathroom and into the living room. She looked at the glass in Charlie's hand, then over to the liquor cabinet. The bottles were there, but no glass for her. "Where's mine, Charlie?" she asked. She already knew the answer.

"You know where the gin is," Charlie said. "Fix me another one, too. Better make a whole jugful while you're at it."

Charlie had every right to be in a foul mood, Linda thought. But it hadn't been her fault. Lawton had done well enough with the writers on Sunday, and there was no reason to suppose he wouldn't carry off the interview as well as Charlie could. To all appearances he was Charlie. Besides, she wasn't Lawton's keeper. Or Charlie's. But there was no point in promoting an argument, particularly with Charlie in his present belligerent mood.

"The man's an idiot," Charlie pronounced. "He's going to ruin my career if this goes on. Jesus Christ on a bicycle, why am I watching Father Knows Best? Turn that thing off for god's sake."

Linda turned off the television, noticing the lack of a 'Baby' or 'Honey.' This was the first time they had had a disagreement. She was seeing an aggressive side of Charlie that was not so pleasant. She thought of Lawton, his gentleness, weakness almost, and wondered whether he had a bad side. He must have. She certainly had. But she didn't want it to come to the fore now. Charlie needed support, not argument. Change the subject, she decided.

She picked up the jug of drinks and sat down beside Charlie on the couch. "Did you have any warning you were going to switch? What did it feel like?"

"Like hell!" Charlie said. "A sort of dizziness like I was going round and round, flushing down the toilet or something. And I could hear that fool Flynn's voice coming through loud and clear. And then there I was with a monkey climbing my frame, smelling like it hadn't changed its socks in seven years."

"Monkeys don't have to change their socks," she said trying to jolly him out of his mood. "And chimpanzees are apes, not monkeys."

"I don't give a crocodile's ass what they are. Flynn set me up, the bastard. He didn't tell me he had a goddam monkey-woman on the show when he booked me. He knows I'm particular who I go on with. No animals and no kids. He knows that. And I'll tell you another thing." He turned to face her. "If all this fartassing around continues, and it looks like it's going to, don't for Crissake let Lawton go near the Tight Owl. I can't afford to have him balls up the act the way he ballsed the Flynn Show."

"But Charlie, I can't stop him if he's determined. You wouldn't let me stop you."

"You're damn right," he cut in savagely.

"Well, it might as well be you. There's no way to tell the difference until something happens to bring Lawton out. Like that man Moore. If he hadn't happened to be talking about Lawton's pet subject everything would have been alright."

"Well, I can't afford to take the risk. You'll have to do something to stop him."

"Don't you think it might stop as suddenly as it started?" She was still trying to head off his aggressiveness.

"Absobloodylutely not. It's getting worse, that's what it's doing. More often. And now I'm getting used to it like it's part of the way of life, know what I mean? I'm not fighting it any more, just wondering when the next time will be. And there's another thing. He doesn't go away between times like he did at first, just seems to be inside here somewhere all the time. He's here now, butting in and trying to tell me what to do."

"What's he telling you?" She sensed she sounded a little too eager for news of Lawton.

"The guy's in love with you. Expects me to do his wooing for him while he's away."

Linda felt her heart skip. And immediately felt disloyal to Charlie, which made her blush.

"O.K, O.K," Charlie said "No problem. You don't owe me anything. I've been fooling around with his secretary. Or I would if he didn't keep popping up at the wrong time."

It was like a slap in the face. She was evidently just one more item in the address book. But then she had no right to complain, wasn't she living with Charlie and falling in love with Lawton? Though Lawton and Charlie were the same person, so was she really being unfaithful?

Charlie cut in on her thoughts. "He figures he's going to do the General Mcarthur bit too."

"What's that mean?"

"He figures he'll be coming back. He's got it worked out, too. He knows this thing isn't going to stop yet. It's got to get worse before it gets better, my mother always used to say."

"What else is he telling you?" she asked, blushing again.

"Miss Nipples is still hot."

"Miss who?"

"He means Miss Saunders. His secretary. She has nipple trouble."

"Sounds more like it's you having the nipple trouble," Linda said tartly. "He hasn't mentioned her."

"He's scared to death of her." Charlie held out his glass for a refill. "I'd love to of seen him when he got back and found her crawling all over him."

"So he got Miss Nipples and you got Maureen?" She giggled. "Serves you right. Bit of a shock for you, wasn't it?"

"Linda Baby, I hope I never get a shock one half as bad as that for the rest of my life. I damn near died of fright, I'm telling you."

"It looked great from a distance. Like part of the show. You being smooched by Maureen and Doctor Moore all tangled up with the Fuchs woman's arms round his neck. It must have been the funniest show Flynn ever did." She was laughing at the memory. "First there were you two chattering away and making him mad, then the chimp pees on the floor and waves at the audience, then the two of you practically get raped on camera, and then to cap it all you teach Maureen to play the pipes. It was hysterical." She was crying with laughter now.

"I had to give her the pipes to get her off me, didn't I?" he said. "Then I couldn't get her to let go of them. Those are six hundred dollar pipes. She did alright though, didn't she?"

"I thought she played better than you, actually, but it's difficult to tell."

"Well thank you for nothing! Let me know when it's to be and I'll tell jokes at your funeral. Which reminds me, I've got a new story idea. Got it from Miss Saunders. She was coming on so hot it was like she had two pussies. Then I had this idea, about the girl with two pussies, nobody liked her because she had such a holier-than-thou manner."

He's got over his bad mood, Linda thought. But I don't know if I can take all these changes much longer, changes of mood, changes of personality, changes of behavior. And changes of heart. Carrying a torch for a man whose real face you've never seen is just crazy. We'll be lucky if we're not all crazy before this is finished. If it ever does finish. Surely it can't just go on and on? And yet if it did all come to a halt and everything got back to normal, would I ever see Lawton again?

* * *

That was a concern that was never far from Lawton's mind. Would he see Linda again? When would it happen? He was looking forward to The Change now. He no longer felt guilty about Linda, unfaithful to Claire. There seemed to have been a change in his whole moral outlook. He couldn't quite pin it down, but it was a lot easier to live with than his old moral code had been. He felt guilty about lowering his standards of behavior and thought, but then excused himself by blaming it on Chesney's influence. Yet the possibility that Chesney might change his whole personality was appalling. Were the two personalities merging? If this went on much longer would they become identical? One person?

Whether it was due to Chesney's influence or not, he found himself better prepared to deal with whatever mood Claire might be in when he let her out of the bathroom. She had drunk only half the pitcher of orange juice, but there had been enough vodka to make her tearfully and remorsefully drunk. Lawton felt only a vague amusement at the trick Chesney had played on Claire, little compassion for her, and no affection. Mostly, he was conscious of a widened gulf between them, a distance as if he were dealing with the ramblings of a drunk he had never met before. He suffered her arms round his neck as she clung to him and cried and told and retold of the long day's miseries, but it was with patience and innate good manners rather than in response to any deeper feeling. The alcohol, and her fear and loneliness, had made her more affectionate than he had known her for a long time. But, while going through the solicitous motions of calming her and petting her, he was surprised by the cold detachment of his mind, which analyzed and criticized and rejected her as if something apart from himself. Maudlin fool, said his mind. Self-centered bitch. Slobbering drunk. She'll be as sullen and demanding as ever by tomorrow.

Yet, in spite of the void where sympathy and affection should have been and an initial revulsion to her cloying kisses, he found himself at last physically responding to her closeness. She had been draped in a damp towel when he found her, but that had quickly fallen unheeded, and as he put his arms round her and rubbed her body to stop the shivering, the masculinity in him was aroused as it had been in the early days of their marriage. He put her to bed and made her hot soup, all the time deriding himself for his weakness. Let her shiver, said a part of his mind. Let her cry for affection. Let her think about her bitchiness. But he was tender and solicitous in spite of himself.

She clung to him as he covered her with the bedclothes. But it was quite definitely Chesney who was saying, "Why waste a body like that, a lay's a lay even if it's your own wife, we promised her something she'd enjoy tonight, remember?"

Lawton resented this new development, this We with which Chesney now combined the two of them into one thought. But, thinking dispassionately of the unclad body in the bed, his mind agreed with Chesney. With a confidence and deliberateness he had never felt before, he undressed and returned to the bed. It was as if Chesney were coaching him. "This is for us, not for her, she'll enjoy it well enough but she doesn't deserve to, this is for us, make the most of it."

It was as if the two of them got into bed beside her and took their pleasure of her.

CHAPTER 12

When Lawton woke the next morning, his first thought was of Linda. His second thought was to check the pictures on the wall. Magazine cutouts. So there had been no Change during the night. He was still at Croftdown Road. He was disappointed, and marveled at the change in himself in such a short time. How many days was it since he had been terrified out of his mind by orange drapes? Did this mean there were to be no more Changes, or only that they would be happening at unexpected times?

For most of the morning, this concern was uppermost in his mind. One problem that seemed to be less pressing, however, was his relationship with Miss Saunders. Possibly as a result of the developing influence of Chesney, he now felt a great deal more confident in dealing with her. But where before his behavior was tempered by loyalty to Claire, this now had been replaced by loyalty to Linda, so he was still determined not to develop any sort of liaison with his secretary. At the same time, at Chesney's prompting, he must make sure she realized the delay might only be temporary.

It was shortly before three that afternoon when the phone in his office made its restrained beeping sound, and Mr. Topham warned him of the imminent arrival of the Chairman of the Board. Not such an inopportune moment as last time, he thought, remembering with some relish Miss Saunders' dash for the door and the remarkable display of anatomy in action. Remembering, yet aware that it had been Chesney sitting in his office chair enjoying the view and not himself.

Rosemary Gwynn entered on a flood tide with the wind astern. This time there seemed to be a subtle difference that Lawton could not quite identify. Not at battle stations today, he noted. Gun decks all cleared away and dressed overall. That's it, he decided, she's dressed differently. Not so forbiddingly. More feminine. And make-up. There's no hiding that five feet ten height to the top-mast, nor the lofty prow, but today she's more statuesque than domineering. And the make-up makes her look positively—good grief! Attractive.

"May I take off my coat, Doctor Wainright?" Miss Gwynn asked in an altogether unusually deferential tone. "It is a little warm in your office."

"Please, Miss Gwynn—er—Mizz Gwynn." Lawton hastened to take her coat from her and was rewarded with a waft of not unpleasant perfume.

She was seated by the time he had hung up the coat. As he passed behind her chair, he looked down over her shoulder, to feel his eyes being drawn into the immeasurable depths of the cavernous cleavage well displayed by a low-cut dress. She looked up, intercepting his gaze, and he blushed in embarrassment at being caught venturing into restricted territory.

She's showing us what no man has ever been permitted to see before, said the voice in his brain. Feel honored. This is one broad who's been scared of losing it all her life, and now she's about to give it to us on a plate with parsley round it.

Go away, damn you, he thought. Don't include me in your lechery. Can't you get it into your head that I'm not like you?

You are me. And I'm you. You can't get away from it, and dear Rosemary's going to make a pass at both of us.

Dear god, I sincerely hope not. This is one time I wish you were here.

I am here. I wouldn't miss this for all the broads on Broadway. Just leave it to me and we'll make out alright.

That's just what I'm afraid of. This is my boss, remember?

All the more reason to treat her right. Incidentally you did a great job with Claire last night.

Lawton blushed again at the memory, sat down behind his desk, found his eyes drawn to the billowy bosom opposite and blushed again.

"I'm glad you have the grace to blush," said Miss Gwynn in her let's-have-a-panty-raid-on-the-men's-dormitory voice. "You made some simply outrageous suggestions yesterday."

"Surely not outrageous, Miss Gwynn? Rather more liberal than an institution of this sort is used to, perhaps. But then we must be progressive, mustn't we?"

"Well, that is exactly the conclusion I reached myself after due consideration." Miss Gwynn crossed her legs and looked down modestly. "It was the apparent—intimacy—of your proposal that rather caught me off guard. It's hardly the sort of proposition a woman in my position is used to."

"I would think a woman as attractive as you would be propositioned all the time, Mizz Gwynn." Don't push me, he almost shouted aloud at Chesney. You'll lose me my job.

It was Miss Gwynn's turn to blush. Lawton noted with interest how the rosy tide ran down her neck to flood out over the broad upper surfaces of her well supported bust, and finally flush down into the cavity between.

Flushing like a toilet, clear down to her navel I betcha. Chesney was still there.

"So you're going to accept my suggestion?" Lawton put his fingertips together and desperately tried to bring some formality back to the conversation. "A woman of your stature—in society—should certainly be represented in the Museum of Woman. I see the Rosemary Gwynn Brassiere as our greatest exhibit."

You can say that again. That's one whopper-topperwobble-stopper I've got to see.

"You make it sound so cold and historical," Miss Gwynn complained. This time it was the please-take-advantage-of-my-frailty voice. "Yesterday I had the distinct impression you felt a rather more personal interest in my cooperation."

"If I gave you that impression, Mizz Gwynn—"

"I think the Mizz is a little formal, don't you?" she interrupted. "Let's make it Rosemary, just within the confines of this office."

"Yes, well. I really must apologize if I sound more formal today. Rosemary." I won't do it! You don't know where all this can lead us. Go away! "I was thinking that we should keep it formal in the office, and then perhaps we could unbend a little over cocktails later?"

Chesney had beaten him. Was it because Chesney's personality was so much stronger than his, or did he really have some sort of death wish to seduce the Chairman of the Board?

"What an excellent suggestion," Miss Gwynn exclaimed delightedly, as if she would never have thought of it herself. "Why don't we make it my place, and I can show it to you. How soon would you like to come?"

I will not go through with this. You and I have different moral standards. You'd seduce your own mother-in-law.

Why not? Older women are more grateful. Besides, I bet Rosie's got hidden depths of passion no man has ever tapped, so let's go find out.

"I have nothing to keep me in the office for the rest of the afternoon," Lawton was aghast to hear himself say. "Why don't we slip away now? No point in delaying a pleasant occasion. I'll get your coat."

Thus it was that shortly after seven bells in the afternoon watch, the Pride of the Fleet sailed proudly into harbor with a reluctant prize in tow. And a snug enough harbor it proved to be. Lawton, alternately sweating with trepidation and seething with fury, could not have imagined such a forceful personality in such delicate surroundings. He had been expected, that much was evident. The bottles were out on a side table beside the couch, and the maid was out visiting a sick mother. Lawton felt the net tightening round him, with Chesney making sure he became deeper enmeshed with every word he spoke.

Miss Gwynn took his overcoat and briefcase, and left him feeling naked and defenseless. Chesney seemed to have left him for once.

He felt like a schoolboy waiting outside the principal's office, fearful and vulnerable.

Miss Gwynn seemed to have matters well in hand. She poured the drinks, and sat beside him on the couch. And in this informal setting, sinking into the cushions instead of towering over him, the outlines of her face softened by the warm lighting and the make-up, the intimacy of her home relaxing the customary stridency of her manner, she seemed to Lawton a woman transformed. There really is something human under that armored carapace, he thought. Was it self consciousness about her height and build that made her behave the way she did? Was she compensating for an imagined lack of femininity by being aggressive and domineering? Was there really any lack, apart from what she imposed upon herself?

He felt, in spite of his resentment at being trapped like a small animal being brought home for her amusement, a sudden empathy for someone who, like himself, lacked confidence with the opposite sex. Except with Linda, of course. Somehow Linda was different. And now, all the indications were that he was about to be unfaithful to Linda. Damn Chesney! It was Chesney who wanted to lay Rosemary Gwynn. Why the devil couldn't he work The Change and come here and do it for himself? But The Change, it seemed, was not programmed to happen on command.

"Let me refill your glass, Lawton," said Rosemary Gwynn. "And then I'll go and fetch the bra for you. That is what you came for, isn't it?"

"Certainly. Yes." He had forgotten about the silly bra in his anxiety about how he was to cope with the advances of this amorous Amazon. A flicker of hope rose inside him. Perhaps that really was all she had in mind, and Chesney was wrong?

Chesney's never wrong about dames. Chicks, broads, floozies, married or single, I know how their minds work, so better relax, we're here for the evening.

When she returned from the next room she had changed out of the dress with the low neckline into a pale yellow pool robe of terry toweling, loosely tied at the waist.

Her feet were bare.

"I just had to get out of those awful shoes," she explained. "When you're my height you can't wear high heels, and those brogues are so unflattering. I thought we might take our drinks out to the jacuzzi."

Lawton's flicker of hope gave up and died. "But—I haven't got anything to wear. And I really can't stop very long. I just came to relieve you of your brassiere."

"That's not a very nice way to talk to a respectable girl," she chided archly. She walked over to the couch and stood in front of him. "I invite you home for cocktails and all you can think about is getting me out of my brassiere. I'm surprised at you, Lawton. Or perhaps I shouldn't be surprised after your behavior yesterday."

"Really, I didn't mean it like that," he stammered. "You said you were going for it. I mean going to fetch it. Look, I really think I'd better be going before I make any more boobs—mistakes."

She laughed, and pushed him firmly back down onto the couch. "I didn't realize you were so sensitive. I can see I shall have to be more careful about kidding you."

He had a sudden memory of Linda beside him in the bed at Park Plaza saying the very same thing. "I was only kidding." But the memory faded. Rosemary Gwynn was standing so close in front of him, and he was so low in the couch, that he had to strain his neck back to look up at her face.

"I've brought the bra out for you," she said "Here." She slipped the pool robe over her shoulders and wriggled her arms out of it, leaving it hanging from the girdle at her waist. "Is this what you wanted?"

As a brassiere it was not unique. It was a half-bra, with wired undercups for support, leaving the breasts bare for wear with a décolleté dress. But as a piece of structural engineering it was a masterpiece, supporting the undersides of two magnificent truncated spheres and thrusting them forward till it seemed they must topple of their own weight.

"Is this what you wanted?" she repeated, standing even closer to him till the twin phenomena were poised alarmingly above him and he could see their pointed tips outlined against the white ceiling. First Miss Saunders, now Miss Gwynn, he thought. Why has my life suddenly become so involved with nipples?

Lawton swallowed hard and tried to think of something appropriate to say. What do you say when your employer threatens to bomb you with twin armor-piercing projectiles, he wondered. He could hardly say he had never wanted her brassiere in the first place, that it was all someone else's idea, that the thought of the fate-worse-than-death this nudity portended filled him with terror. He needed a drink, but his head was tilted skyward and nothing seemed to be able to bring it down. He opened his mouth. As if from a distance he heard his own voice say enthusiastically, "Rosie Baby, forget the brassiere. Those are the greatest knockers I've seen in a long career of tit-fancying. How come you've hid 'em all this time?"

"One doesn't exactly flaunt them in polite society," Miss Gwynn replied primly.

"Flaunt 'em all you want at me, Baby. Right now I'm about as far from polite society as you're ever likely to get. Take a stroll around the room and let an expert view the action."

"Well, my goodness Doctor Wainright!" Miss Gwynn was only slightly more amazed than Lawton. "You certainly are appreciative. And expressive. I really didn't expect the sight of—knockers, as you call them—to affect you quite like this. What a deep one you are, indeed! Do you really think this will be suitable for your exhibit? Perhaps you'd better look at it more closely. I'll take it off for you. We don't want it to get wet in the jacuzzi, do we?"

She moved back a step and felt for the fastening.

Lawton's eyes followed her, then looked away quickly. How, he wondered, would he ever be able to face the Chairman of the Board at future meetings? He looked down at the glass in his hand and drained it quickly.

"I'll drink to that, Rosie Baby," said the enthusiastic voice that could never have been his own.

"Oh, I'm so sorry!" she exclaimed. "How thoughtless of me. Let me get you another." She leaned over to pick the glass from off the coffee table beside him, and the miracle of structural support threatened to become a fall-out disaster.

"For god's sake keep those things under control," gasped Lawton, and this time it was his own voice. "Before they do some damage," added Chesney. "Those things are a hazard to navigation."

Miss Gwynn took the empty glass and refilled it, pouring one for herself at the same time. "Let's drink to the Museum of Woman," she said brightly. "I think it was a marvelous idea of yours. Now, why don't we move out to the jacuzzi? I've changed already." She put her glass down on the table.

Watching Lawton's face, she unhooked the brassiere and dropped it onto his lap. "There, that's for the Museum," she said. Then, pulling at the girdle round her waist she loosened it and let the pool-robe fall to her feet. "And this is for you, Doctor Wainright. Now let's get you changed. You can't get into the jacuzzi like that, can you?"

She bent over Lawton and began to unbutton his shirt.

"No!" he shouted, panic-stricken. "Not now. I can't. Please, Miss Gwynn. You don't understand." His glass fell to the floor as he struggled with the strong hands that were already unbuckling his belt. "Miss Gwynn, it's all a misunderstanding. It wasn't really my idea at all."

She put one hand on his chest and pushed him hard down into the cushions, holding him there while her other hand took hold of his zipper. "I knew there were men who deceived women into inviting them home and then forced them to undress and attacked them," she said grimly. "I don't think the members of the Board would be impressed to learn that you are one of those men, Doctor Wainright."

"I most certainly am not." Lawton was struggling to get her hand off his zipper. "I wouldn't even know how to deceive a woman in the first place."

"Then how do you account for my having to defend myself against you in this way? It's very fortunate I'm strong enough to be able to subdue you. You're a positive animal.

I really think the Board would take a very serious view of this if I were to tell them."

"That's blackmail." This woman had hidden depths of depravity, he decided. "You wouldn't do that?"

"I most certainly would, Doctor Wainright," She smiled down at him triumphantly. "Are you going to give up?"

He was powerless under her weight, but she took his lack of opposition for acquiescence and pulled his hand away from his zipper. This can't be happening to me, he thought, as he felt her fingers where no Chairman of the Board's fingers should ever be. He felt faint. Her face began to blur above him. Dizziness overtook him, till he seemed to be revolving in a vortex that threatened to drag him down into the depths of the couch.

Then he heard the voice, Chesney's voice, loud and clear. "The Marines are coming, don't give up the ship, shipmate." The weight was no longer pressing on his chest, the dizziness was gone, and more urgently so were the groping fingers that threatened his very self respect.

CHAPTER 13

The echo of Chesney's voice was still in his ears, "Don't give up the ship, shipmate!" The only other sound was the air conditioning above Lawton's head. The dizziness was gone, so he opened his eyes. He recognized the cluttered comfort of Chesney's den at the Park Plaza, the litter of paper on the desk, and the posters and photographs on the wall. He felt guiltily for his zipper. No breach of integrity there. But of course, this was not his zipper anyway, not his clothes. He was in Chesney's apartment, dressed in Chesney's clothes. Until the next Change he was Chesney. It must be Chesney who at this very moment was fighting for his honor in the lair of the Dragon Lady. And yet it seemed unlikely, really, that Chesney would be putting up much of a fight.

Linda was going to be home later than usual, he remembered, though how or why he remembered he couldn't say. Linda had to go to her own apartment on the way home from work. He was doubly glad she was still staying on at Park Plaza, mainly because he could hardly wait to see her again, but also because he doubted his sanity could survive the Changes much longer without someone to give him support. He thought of Chesney, not only with no one to confide in but with Claire to cope with when he got home. However, he seemed to be making the most of his opportunities. But how long would he be able to go on before the strain began to tell? He was a strong character, not a particularly likable one, but a strong one.

As the evening wore on and his anxiety to see Linda increased, Lawton realized he was not losing his identity as he had before. So the Change was still evolving? What might the next phase be? Complete dual personality? God forbid! The strain was already having its effect on him. It was not any more the trauma of the transfer itself, but the way the course and style of his life were being altered out of all recognition. Things were happening to him he could never have dreamed of. Alarming things. And at an alarming rate. Was this the way Chesney lived, what his normal life was like?

There was still half an hour to kill before Linda could possibly be home. The monologue could do with tightening, he decided. The rambling style was good, but it should be tighter. Too bad the management insisted on keeping the act clean. Well, fairly clean. There were so many more things he could work in if it was wide open. Too bad he wasn't playing the Woolly Lamb Club, though he didn't much care for gay audiences. He looked at himself in the mirror over the desk. The grey hairs were no worse. If anything he seemed to be looking younger. Hair needed cutting soon, or he'd be another Wainright. Take off a bit of weight and grow a mustache and they weren't too dissimilar.

Strange that it wasn't possible to tell what was going on in Rosemary Gwynn's apartment. Chesney seemed to have been looking over his shoulder all day. Perhaps his subconscious was butting in on Chesney even now. Strange the way Miss Gwynn had responded to Chesney's fooling. Who would have thought she was so hungry? Not a bad looking broad. Particularly when she was stripped for action. But that blackmail line was ominous. It meant she'd be back for more whenever the mood took her.

He heard the key in the front door, and his heart leaped. How should he greet Linda? Would he have to tell her or would she guess? And would she be pleased it was him? She was Chesney's girl after all, and he really had no right to expect her to be in love with him the way he was with her. As she came into the room, running her hand through her hair and tossing her head in the way he already knew so well, he was standing in the middle of the room. She looked at him and said nothing. Neither of them spoke. He opened his arms to her and she came across the room to him, her eyes lighting up in a smile that was like a spring crocus opening in the morning sun. She came into his arms, and this time it was he who led the way, with no shyness or hesitation, pressing her close and stroking her hair and pouring his whole being into her as they kissed.

She stood passive for a few moments, accepting everything he gave and surrendering to him. Then her arms tightened about him and he felt her entering him, becoming a part of him. When they paused for breath she was smiling with eyes filled with tears.

"You could tell?" he asked.

"Of course, I knew right away."

"How did you know? Do we look different?"

"I can't tell you, my darling. I think I could feel you here as soon as I opened the front door, but I wouldn't let myself hope. Was it bad this time?"

"No," he said. "It's getting easier. I've been hoping it would happen ever since yesterday."

"So have I. It's getting so I watch Charlie all the time just in case. I try not to let him see but he knows, I'm sure."

"He couldn't care less. About losing you, I mean. By now he should have added Miss Gwynn's cherry to his collection."

"I thought it was Miss Saunders. Who's Miss Gwynn?"

"The Chairman of the Board. My boss. He laid the groundwork yesterday, and today she came in with smoke pouring out of her pants and made a pretty fair attempt at raping me."

"Was she successful?" Linda took his hand and headed toward the bedroom.

"Damn nearly. She's built like a Marine drill sergeant on a vitamin diet. It was only a matter of time. But then everything went hazy and I assume he took over because I'm here."

"I'm glad he got there in time, lover," she said. "If anyone's going to rape you I'd like to think you can enjoy it. I'm going to take a shower first. Want to join me?"

It was later that evening that the argument began, the argument that was to develop into their first row. Lawton had showered for the second time, and called out for a drink while he was dressing before going to the club.

"Charlie asked me to try to stop you going to the club," Linda said diffidently when she brought the gin and tonic into the bedroom.

"The hell he did! What's it got to do with him?" he demanded truculently.

"Well, it's his act."

"He's scared I'll screw it up? Listen Baby, I've got some changes in mind to really make that act take off. He's not telling me what to do."

She had warned Charlie it would be impossible to stop him, and she was reluctant to get into an argument about it. But she could see the very real danger of something going wrong. She felt she owed it to Charlie to keep trying.

"It's not that you can't do it. But you know as well as I do some sort of Change might happen in the middle."

"Linda, you're bugging me," he shouted at her. "Just drop it, will you? I don't give a tom-tit's turd what he says. He's playing merry hell with everything of mine he touches anyway."

She dropped it, but she felt miserable at the way he was reacting. It was not really Lawton yelling at her, she knew, but it hurt all the same. She wanted to grab him and shake him, shake Charlie right out of him till he sounded like Lawton again, but she was frightened of how he might react in his present mood. He was calling for another drink. Charlie always put away several gins before leaving for the club, but Linda was concerned about the way they might affect Lawton. He had drunk four gins, and she was reluctant to bring him any more.

"Darling, you're not used to drinking so much," she began, but he cut her off.

"You think someone's appointed you my nursemaid or something?" he snarled. "Quit pushing me around, Linda. I can do without it. I can do without any of this hassle."

As soon as she spoke she knew it was a mistake. But once the words were out there was no recalling them. "You'll have to get your own, then. I'm not bringing you any more. I don't want to be responsible."

He was putting keys and money away into his pockets. He turned away from the dressing table and looked coldly at her. Deliberately he took a ten-dollar bill out of his wallet, and threw it on the floor in front of her.

"You don't need to feel responsible for me. You didn't buy me. Here's your ten bucks back. It was a bad investment, Baby. Ten bucks or ten million, you don't buy the right to tell Charlie Chesney what goes and what doesn't. Buy yourself a cab fare home."

He pushed past her, and a moment later she heard the front door of the apartment slam.

By the time Lawton arrived at the club the image of Linda's stricken face as he left the room was blotting out all other conscious thought from his mind. It was as if the car had found its own way, and parked itself. He was not aware of driving or parking the car, or of striding into the club and brushing aside the group of fans at the door as he made straight for his dressing room. The face was all he could remember. There was a fog over all that had gone before. He knew there had been a row, that he must have hurt her badly, but what he had said or what had led to it was blotted from his memory.

Urgently he picked up the phone and dialed the number of his apartment. He must talk to her, explain that it must have been Chesney speaking, not him. He let the phone ring and ring but there was no answer, and he finally gave up.

He put the phone down, then picked it up again and dialed the bar and ordered a pitcher of gin and tonics.

Everything was falling to pieces around him, it seemed. His marriage hardly seemed likely to survive much longer. His relationships at the museum were jeopardizing his position there, and his career. His mind was being occupied by an alien presence. And now it seemed the only stable component had been wrecked.

Funny thing, he thought—funny peculiar, not funny ha-ha—that he should have come to regard an affair with someone who only existed in his fantasy life as the only stable component in his life. Linda had been his storm anchor. Her presence and her help were all that kept him from going out of his mind. Possibly he was already out of his mind. He must be to do what he had done tonight.

"Buy yourself a cab-fare home," he had said. It came to him clearly now. The one remark most likely to hurt her and drive her away.

The waiter arrived with his pitcher, and automatically he signed his name on the bill. Charlie. That was all he ever signed. Everyone knew him. Cheerful Charlie Chesney. He filled the glass and swilled it down. God, I needed that, he thought, pouring another. Who does the bitch think she is? No one tells Charlie Chesney what to do. Seems like all the women I get, they're either just along for the free ride or else they want to do the driving.

By show time, the pitcher was empty. He was aggressively drunk. He had a grudge against everyone. It was more than he could do to remember what the grudge was, but it seemed like a good idea to insult everyone. Including the club manager, the bandleader, a small group of the producer's friends seeking his autograph and a radio reporter.

The act usually began with a song and ended with the monologue, and that fact alone was enough to make him decide to open with the monologue. After accepting the opening applause, he climbed onto the high stool from which he normally faced the audience, put his foot where there was no rung, and fell heavily to the floor. The audience, mostly members of a computer salesmen's conference, thought it hilarious. He resented the laughter, and replied with an obscene gesture of Gaelic origin involving the forearm and index finger, at which the audience laughed even more. There was a moment's silence during which he climbed back onto the stool and tried to remember why he was so drunk. But the audience was waiting.

"Ladies and gentlemen," he began, "though I use the description with some reservation. Half the gentlemen here tonight are cheating on their wives. The other half just wish they were. Ladies, on the other hand, don't cheat. Half the ladies here tonight are simply helping the men to cheat. The other half don't intend to cooperate, but the men don't find out till later that they've been cheated.

Now, I'm going to let you into a little secret. Ready? The reason I'm in such a bloody mood tonight is, this act, the one you're watching right now, this absolutely excellent act which everyone knows is the best in town, is really a double act. Cheerful Charlie Chesney is really two people, a double identity. No kidding. Not both at the same time, of course. You'll never know which one of us you're looking at. One night it may be Charlie. Another night it may be Lawton. We look exactly the same as each other, but Lawton's a wimp and Charlie's a rotten bugger. You have to know them to tell which is which. So, ladies and gentlemen—and I won't go into all that again—you're getting a double act for the price of a single."

It was at this point that he fell off the stool again. There was no laughter this time. As the act progressed it became obvious that Cheerful Charlie Chesney was far from cheerful, and more nearly unpleasantly drunk. Many of the audience left. The final applause was minimal. Immediately after the show he lurched out of the club and hailed a taxi, foggily aware that he had bombed, and resentful of the audience for causing it.

Lawton awoke the next morning to find himself on the bed fully clothed. He had been dreaming that he was back at Croftdown Road, but the familiar sourness in his mouth warned him he was not to escape the consequences of the previous night. He felt very ill.

If only last night could have been a dream. Groggily he reached out for Linda, but her side of the bed was empty. So it had really happened. He had sent her away. Fury at Chesney rose within him. It had been Chesney who threw the ten dollars at her, told her to buy a cab-fare home. Chesney who had ruined his own act at the Tight Owl. It was Chesney's life, certainly, but Chesney had no right to make a mess of it while Lawton had to share it. And he had no right to come between Lawton and Linda.

Linda would be up by now, getting ready to leave for the ad agency. She would be waiting for him to phone her, surely? She must realize it had been Chesney talking and not him. He would persuade her and she would move back in. She must. She couldn't blame him for Chesney's oafishness. Not if she really loved him. He had better phone right away, before Chesney started taking over again.

Shakily he dialed her number. There was no answer to the first four rings, then at last he heard her voice.

"Good morning." The crisp way she always answered the phone.

"Linda darling, I was afraid I'd missed you."

"Lawton? Hallo my darling. I was hoping you'd call."

"I was hoping you'd be hoping. Linda, you're not going to stay away? You can't. You know it wasn't me last night."

"I know, darling. It was beastly, wasn't it? I didn't know Charlie could be like that."

"You'll come back tonight?"

"Lawton dear, it's not as easy as that. How do I know you'll be there tonight?"

He had no answer for her. This was a problem that had not entered his head. Linda was right, they could change at any time.

"I can't go back to living with Charlie. I don't want to anyway, after last night. That's all over. And even if you were there the same sort of thing could happen again at any time. You keep switching personalities, the two of you, all the time. It's like living with two different people at the same time."

"But Linda!" He was shouting, frantic at the thought of losing her. "You're not going to just stay away? I want you. I love you. Don't you want to be with me?"

"More than anything, my darling. More than ever now. But I can't see any way it'll work. I've spent most of the night thinking about it, trying to find a way. Charlie doesn't want me there any more, and anyway the only reason I really wanted to stay was to be there when you came. Even if we meet somewhere we can never be sure he won't take over like he did last night, and spoil everything. He's always there now, a part of you."

"Can't you risk that?"

"No." Her voice was suddenly flat. "I'm not going through another row like that. Think about it, Lawton. If we go for a drink together he's likely to suddenly pop up. Even if he stays out of the conversation I'll always be wondering whether he's going to take over, or even worse whether you're going to change into him. If I go to bed with you, do you think I want to suddenly find myself making love to him instead? Even now, on the phone, I'm expecting him to start yelling at me any minute. Do you think I haven't spent hours thinking about it, trying to find a way?"

Lawton felt sick. More sick than just from the hangover. During the past few days of upheaval the one steady support in all the madness had been Linda. And now he was losing her. There would be nothing to look forward to each time, nothing to make the Change bearable. Even Claire was going away to stay with her Aunt Alice. Back in Croftdown Road he would be completely alone. Completely alone! Of course!"

"I've got it, Linda," he shouted excitedly. "Claire's going away. I shall be alone. You can come and stay at Croftdown Road with me. Or I can come to your place."

"Darling, I want it as much as you do, believe me, but don't you see it's just the same wherever we are? We can never be sure you're not going to change. If we knew we could have a complete day together, or even a few hours. But it's happening more often now. It could happen any time. Besides . . ."

"What?"

"I'm frightened. I'm not sure I'd really find you at Croftdown Road. I'm still not sure you really exist at all when you're not here. I'm not sure I want to find out."

"That's crazy!" he scoffed, forgetting his own similar fears about her.

"Lawton, I think maybe I am crazy. I don't know whether I'm imagining this whole thing myself. I'm beginning to wonder if this isn't all in my own mind. I never know who I'm coming home to, who I'm waking up to in the morning, even whether you'll stay the same for a few minutes on end. I really wonder whether this is actually happening, or whether I'm cracking up myself."

He would have pleaded with her all day, but she knew she had to be firm. When she hung up on his pleading she knew she was never going to see him again. She was not going to have a nervous breakdown over a man whose real face she might never see, who might not even exist. She was not even going to cry. Then she rushed to the bedroom and flung herself on the bed, and cried till there was no more feeling left in her. Throughout the day she tried not to think about him. But some time during the afternoon she knew she was going to have to find out, once and for all. She would have to get herself a map of the city and find out whether Croftdown Road really existed. If it did she would have to take the ultimate step.

Lawton put down the phone, oblivious of the nausea of his hangover, knowing for the first time in his life how it felt to seriously consider suicide. There could be no reason to endure this nonsensical alternation between the ruins of a marriage and career and the chimera of a fantasy life, when neither existence could include Linda. Till then, suicide had always seemed the coward's solution, the easy way of evading responsibility. When it was someone else's misery it was so easy to pontificate. Now that it was his misery it made sense to do away with a life that held no future.

This mood was abruptly interrupted by the ringing of the phone. It was the manager of the Tight Owl, calling to tell Charlie his contract was cancelled.

CHAPTER 14

When Charlie Chesney awoke that same morning it was not, as so often, with a hangover. He was alone, in the guestroom, and he could remember quite clearly why. Claire was already in bed when he had arrived home the night before. She had refused to talk to him, other than to order him out of her bedroom. He had no idea what time it was. He had been in no hurry to leave the comfort of Rosemary Gwynn's bed, though it had required considerable stamina to stay. Although the novelty had quickly worn off, there had been a certain perverse satisfaction in satisfying her demands until the last dog was hung.

A bitch in heat's not in the same class as our little Rosie, he decided. That broad can't have had it since before I found out pussy wasn't something that scratched.

So the morning at Croftdown Road inevitably began with acrimony. Claire was already up when he emerged from the guestroom and headed for the bathroom.

"Lawton, we've got to have a talk," she called from the bedroom. "I'm not putting up with this kind of thing any longer."

"Right," he said affably. "Talk away. I'll go clean my teeth."

"You'll do nothing of the sort. I'm not going to shout at you through the bathroom door. You can clean your teeth afterwards."

"After what, dear?" he asked innocently.

"After I've—after we've finished talking." She was standing by her dressing table, shapeless in a baggy green tracksuit, hair in curlers and her mouth set in a grim line. "Lawton, I will not be treated like this. Am I your wife or not?"

"You certainly sound like it, dear."

"Then you owe me more consideration than to come in at half past two in the morning. And you knew I needed the car last night. I had to take a taxi."

"I hope you gave it back," he said. "You could get in trouble."

"This is no time to be facetious. I don't believe you care about me at all. You give me no consideration whatsoever. What were you doing last night? I phoned your office and you weren't there. You were out with that woman, weren't you?"

"Which woman?" he asked, deliberately provocative.

"Your new secretary. Miss Whatsername."

"Saunders," he prompted. "No, I wasn't with Miss Saunders. As a matter of fact I was with the Chairman of the Board. Charming lady. Thinks the world of me." He sat on the bed and looked up at her as if he were seeing her for the first time.

"What's got into you, Claire? You've been acting like a dog without fleas for months. Years. Seems like years, anyway. You're bitchy, you're demanding, and you're about as lovable as a gopher with a dose of clap."

"You disgusting beast," she spat at him, and began to cry.

"I haven't finished yet," he said, ignoring her tears. "The only time you've been civil in months was the other night, and that was only because you were frightened and wanted sympathy."

"That was horrible," she sobbed. "You can't imagine how awful it was to be locked in the bathroom all day. You were nice to me then. Why can't you always be like that? We hadn't been to bed together like that for ever so long."

"We go to bed together every night."

"Not like that."

"You mean for screwing?"

"Lawton, must you be so crude? You know I don't like that kind of talk."

She looks so bloody stupid, he thought, standing there looking like a fish-wife on a Friday night and making like Lady Muck at a garden party.

"I know you don't like it," he said. "I know only too well exactly what you like and what you don't like. And what you want and what you don't want. You're always telling me. Your conversation contains very little else. Have you any idea what I like, or doesn't it matter?"

"I always try to consider your wants, Lawton," she sobbed in a hurt tone. "You've only got to tell me."

"Right, I'll tell you what I want right now," He bared his teeth in a snarl and reached out to grab her. She shrieked and backed away from him.

"Don't you dare! Don't you dare touch me. I don't know what's come over you in the last few days. You used to be a gentleman."

"You used to be a wife," he countered. "Now all you can think of is having what you want when you want it. You know what you seem like to me? You seem like a wife who's got something going on the side."

She colored, and looked at him wide-eyed. "How dare you say such a thing? It's more like you're playing around. What about that Miss Saunders?"

"What about her?"

"Are you seeing her?"

"Sure. I see her every day. She's my secretary."

"You know what I mean. Have you kissed her yet?"

"She won't let me kiss it in the office."

"Kiss what in the office?"

"Her yet. She's very conservative. Crazy about politics. Always ready to join a good party. But you changed the subject very neatly just now. What about you? Are you sure you're not having a bit on the side?"

"That's a cheap and nasty thing to say," she shouted at him, flushing till the fire reached up to the roots of her flaming hair.

"Don't get your knickers in a knot, Baby," he grinned. "It just seemed to me the other night at the Tight Owl there was something going between you and that Cheerful Charlie Chesney. You sure you haven't been having it off with him?"

She laughed, relieved. "Charlie Chesney? What a silly idea. I'd never seen him before. Besides, he's not my type."

"I guess not," he said dryly. "He's rather like me to look at, and certainly I don't seem to be your type." He got up. "I've got to be getting dressed. But I'm going to be watching you, Baby. If you've got something going on the side I shall find out."

Seemed to touch her on a raw spot, he thought, as he went into the bathroom. So she's playing around? That might explain why she's so intolerant of me. Not that I could give a fish's tit what she does any more.

She came out of the bedroom just as he was leaving, and stood by the front door.

"Don't forget I'm going to stay with Aunt Alice today," she reminded him. "I'll call you in a few days and let you know when I'm coming home."

"Have a nice time dear," he said ironically, and leaned over to kiss her cheek.

"Your breath smells terrible." She fanned the air with her hand. "You've been drinking again."

"It's the new mouthwash, dear. Scotch flavored, for that seductive he-man morning-after fragrance that women can't resist. Made by the same people who make Pepsodent flavored Scotch for the man who can't brush between drinks."

As he drove to the museum Charlie's lighthearted veneer began to peel. Quite early in life he had developed the facade of buffoonery and facetiousness that seemed to be expected of a professional comedian. But there were times when he was alone and the cliches and the facile repartee deserted him, and dull depression took hold. This was going to be one of those times. The Changes were getting worse. More often, for one thing. For another, it seemed that he was no longer losing his own awareness as he had on the earlier occasions. He knew he was Charlie, but he was Lawton too, and every action and decision was subject to the conflicting emotions and principles of both of them. Was this what split personality was all about? In spite of the conclusions he and Linda had reached, was he really out of his mind?

He could do without these daily frictions with Claire, too. It must be bad enough for Lawton, but Lawton deserved whatever he got with his "Yes dear, no dear." This was precisely why he had never married, never let himself be trapped into a permanent life with one woman who might or might not stay amenable forever. He could do without that sort of hassle. But now he was having to put up with it from someone else's wife! And all the time that cement head was making time with his girl, ruining his act, wrecking his career.

By the time he reached the parking lot he was feeling better. The architect was coming to discuss the plans for reconstruction of the old wing, the new catalog would be in, there was a staff meeting at ten, and the President of the Archaeological Society was coming to present a check to the museum. It was going to be a full day.

It was so full, in fact, that there was no time to dwell on the problems that had been occupying him on the way into town. And in contrast to the acrimonious beginning, the day went smoothly and pleasantly. It was not until the bell announced the five o'clock closing hour, and Miss Saunders came into the office to report the establishment cleared, that more personal matters began to come to the fore. Miss Saunders had not been so intrusive. Or perhaps the word was protrusive, he thought. At any rate, her clothes were less figure hugging today, and there had been no personal overtures. True, the smile was not quite so bright, and that was a pity. The kid deserves a break, Charlie thought.

"Thank you, Miss Saunders," he said in answer to the report. "It will be nice to relax after a busy day. Are you planning on going straight home, or can I persuade you to stop off for a cocktail or two?"

Miss Saunders' face lit up. "I haven't got anything on tonight, Doctor Wainright."

Charlie toyed with a suitable reply, and decided the question of whether she had anything on could wait till later. By then she wouldn't have, with any luck.

"Great!" he said. "You've got your car? Why don't you follow me? Mine's the black Mazda."

It would have made sense to tell her where they were going, in case she lost him in the traffic, but there might be some argument if he told her they were going to his house. In the event, she stuck close to his tail. They drove into Croftdown Road together, and she parked behind him outside the house. To hell with the neighbors, he thought. If they talk about it to Claire it'll give her something else to bitch about.

"Claire's away for a few days," he explained as he opened the front door. "While the cat's away the mice can have a nibble, eh?"

She looked round her with interest as he took her coat. "There's that fixation on nipples again," she accused, smoothing her dress and wishing she had worn one of the tight sweaters. "I was beginning to think you'd lost interest in them."

"I was beginning to think you'd got rid of them," he countered. "Where are they?"

"All present and correct. It's just a matter of the right kind of bra."

"Come on into the living room," he said. "I'll fix you a drink. Do you have another name? I can't go on calling you Miss Saunders."

"Why not?"

"Doesn't seem to fit. 'What beautiful nipples you have, Miss Saunders.' Or, 'Come into the bedroom and take off your clothes, Miss Saunders.' What do your friends call you?"

"Sam. Short for Samantha. What do your friends call you?"

"Charlie." He corrected himself quickly. "Lawton, really."

"Don't you know?"

"Charlie's my middle name. Call me Lawton."

"And Claire's your wife?"

"You could call her that. You'd have to stretch the ima-gination, though."

"Don't you get on?"

"She thinks I'm Quasimodo. The only reason she doesn't go home to Mother is her mother can't stand her. That and to punish me. What'll you drink? Gin and tonic, sherry, snoo?"

"What's snoo?"

"Nothing. What's snoo with you?"

"Oh, come on now," she laughed. "I heard that on MASH years ago."

"What d'you expect? I'm an archaeologist, not a comedian. I dig them up years after other people have thrown them away. What's your pleasure?"

"Don't tempt me, Lawton. We can all be comics. Sherry will be nice. What did Miss Gwynn want yesterday?"

"She wanted to take me home to bed."

"Be serious."

"I fantasize a lot."

"You must do. Do you fantasize about me?"

Charlie looked at her over his glass. "All the time, Baby. You wouldn't believe the fantasies I have about you."

"How exciting!" she exclaimed. "I've never been in anyone's fantasies before. Tell me about them."

"Which one will you have? Pirate captain takes innocent young girl prisoner and carries her away to a fate worse than death, or depraved boss entices secretary home and makes her his sex slave?"

She drained her drink carefully and looked at him in wide-eyed innocence. "The fate worse than death sounds awfully exciting, but I think the sex-slave one for now. We could always keep the pirate one for another time, couldn't we?"

"You got yourself a deal, Sam baby," said Charlie, taking her by the hand. "The bedroom's this way,"

CHAPTER 15

It had not been a good day for Lawton Wainright. After the initial frenetic reaction to the call from the club manager canceling his contract, he had calmed down and nursed his hangover for an hour. He tried to remember what Linda had put in the pick-me-up she had prepared on Sunday. Flaming Onion, she had called it. He settled for a Horse's Neck, and ruined it by putting too much ginger ale in the brandy. He wondered whether his agent had heard the news. It must be all round town. Soon the reporters would be calling for a story. He dialed Marvin's number, but the secretary told him coldly that Mr. Helpman was out of town for the day. He thought of calling the Woolly Lamb and a couple of other clubs, but he was already in enough trouble without alienating his agent.

When at last he slumped down in front of the television, there was nothing but hash on the screen. And that left the liquor cabinet. Throughout the day they fought with one another, Charlie's bitter resentment overlaid with maudlin self-pity, and Lawton's awareness that he must stay sober in case Linda might take it into her head to come back. By six o'clock that evening, the victory was Charlie's, and for the second time in two days Lawton experienced the unique—for him—sensation of being totally drunk.

So, with his head already spinning, there was nothing to indicate that the sudden violent increase was anything more than one of the hangover pleasures Chesney seemed to crave. Then he heard the voice, Miss Saunders' voice, as if it had been close beside his left ear. It was whispering, urgently. "Don't stop, master. Do anything you like to your slave but please don't stop now."

He had closed his eyes against the spinning room. When he opened them the dizziness was gone, and so were all the horrid side effects of Chesney's self-indulgence. He felt well, extremely well. So well, in fact, that at that very moment a most exquisite sensation was rising to a peak of ecstasy. A gentle perfume was in his nostrils, but he was in no condition to investigate the source. The exquisite sensation he recognized well enough, though he could have wished there was more time to recognize it before it reached it's climax and was gone. A gentle tongue began to probe his ear, and then Miss Saunders' voice again.

"What does my master wish of his slave?"

The perfume, he discovered, emanated from a pool of corn-colored hair into which his nose was pressed. The tongue, it seemed, also belonged to Miss Saunders, though he could hardly swear to it since it had never, so far as he knew, been in his ear before.

Memory was returning as he raised himself on his elbows to look into the radiant face of his secretary. His first instinct was to apologize. To Lawton Wainright, it was hardly seemly that the administrator of the Museum of Anthropology should be reclining naked atop his equally naked secretary. But on second thoughts, what was there really to apologize for? This was presumably what Miss Saunders had been striving for since her first day in the office. He would certainly not have countenanced such conduct had it been left up to him, but fortunately the decision had been taken out of his hands. Very fortunately.

"That was a beautiful fantasy," Miss Saunders purred. "But you never asked me about mine. I've been having one all week. Can we try mine now, please?"

It was at that moment that Linda McClusky, having located Croftdown Road on the street map, and with considerable trepidation having decided to take the ultimate step and find out whether or not Lawton Wainright really existed, pulled up outside the Wainright house. All the way out she had been rehearsing what she would say, how she would react, preparing herself for the worst. The worst would be that there was no Lawton Wainright living there. Or, if there was a Lawton Wainright living there, he would deny knowing her. It might, of course, be Charlie who opened the door. That would be a disappointment, but at least she would know what she wanted to know, that the Changes really were happening and Lawton was more than just a fantasy in her own mind.

There was no answer when she rang the bell. That seemed strange, because there were two cars parked outside the house. She rang again, determined to wake the neighborhood if necessary now that she had finally found the courage to come. A taxi pulled up, and double-parked beside her car. She watched the passenger get out and pay the driver. Not a salesperson. Too smartly dressed. Attractive if she could learn to smile, particularly with that shock of startling red hair.

"Hullo," she said, as the stranger walked up the pathway to the door. "There doesn't seem to be anyone home. I've been ringing."

Claire Wainright looked her over suspiciously. "Who do you want to see?" she asked.

"I'm wondering if a Doctor Wainright lives here," Linda said, dreading the answer.

"I'm Mrs. Wainright." Claire said. "Doctor Wainright does live here. Who are you?"

All day the idea that Lawton must have been with some woman the night before had been festering in Claire's mind. Charlie had been nearer the mark than he realized with his challenge of her own fidelity, but she saw no reason why her husband should be allowed to cheat on her. His behavior had been strange ever since the previous Saturday. There could be only one reason in her mind. All day suspicion mouldered and grew, feeding on imagination.

"I've just remembered something I need to do," she had told her Aunt Alice, and called the taxi company. "I'll be back in an hour or so."

She had intended to cruise by the house to see if Lawton was at home, then come back later for the coup-de-grace. But events were evidently moving faster than she expected, for already an attractive girl was at the door. Miss Saunders? There was one way to find out. She paid off the taxi and marched purposefully up the path.

"I'm Mrs. Wainright," she said, with venom in her voice. "Doctor Wainright does live here. Who are you?"

She can't know about me, Linda thought. Lawton hasn't talked to her about the Change. "I'm Doctor Wainright's secretary," she lied. "Something came up after he left."

Claire smiled, exultant at her prescience. "I've been looking forward to meeting you, Miss Saunders. Do come inside." She turned the key and pushed the door open, standing aside to let Linda enter first. Linda hesitated.

"He doesn't seem to be here," she said weakly. "There's no need to bother you, thanks anyway."

"Oh, you must come in," Claire insisted, altogether too sweetly. She hugged herself in satisfaction. So her hunch was right. It was the secretary, and she certainly hadn't expected a wife to complicate the assignation. "If he's not in now he can't be far away. The car's outside."

Linda's reply was interrupted by a shriek of laughter from somewhere in the house. Claire's eyes looked uncertainly from Linda to the source of the sound, and back to Linda. Then quickly she swung round and ran through the hall. This has got to be something else, Linda thought. I'm not going to miss this. This has just got to be Charlie Chesney in action. I can't imagine it being Lawton.

She followed Claire through the house. The laughter was continuous now, and louder. Claire reached the bedroom door, which was half-open. She pushed it wide, and Linda stood beside her looking in at the confusion of limbs and entangled nakedness that writhed and heaved on the bed. There were hairy legs that must presumably belong to Charlie, but the face belonging to them was nowhere to be seen. Muffled noises of a vaguely masculine nature were erupting from somewhere beneath what, even to Linda's prejudiced eye, was a singularly well rounded rump. And various shrieks and giggles and other indications of enjoyment came from the general direction of a tousled mass of corn-colored hair.

To Linda, though she was not particularly experienced in such orgiastic romping, there seemed to be something altogether wrong. The masculine noises, far from expressing ecstatic delight, were staccato and remonstrative, almost as if the male half of the entanglement would prefer to be somewhere else. To Claire, whose upbringing and experience had not prepared her for the fact that such gymnastic contortions were even possible, particularly between members of different sexes, the display was at the very least disgusting. And since it was presumably her husband who made up one half of the inosculating embranglement it was more than disgusting. It was a matter of principle.

Linda was never quite sure what her reaction might have been in Claire's place. In the event, there was no doubt in Claire's mind as to what she should do first. Advancing swiftly to the bed, she reached over and delivered a ringing slap to the reciprocating rump, a slap that instantly brought a rosy glow to the receiving cheek and a yelp of agony from the other end of the bed. At least we know those two parts belong to each other, Linda thought objectively. Once more Claire's hand connected, and even to Linda, who had no quarrel with the owner of the beleaguered buttock, it was a palpable hit, a hit it was a pleasure to be associated with, however remotely.

This time the rump shot into the air, the body rolled over onto its back, and the corn-colored hair framed a face that registered fury, indignation, puzzlement, and finally consternation. Linda could have felt sympathy for the girl, had not the reluctant body underneath apparently belonged to Lawton. Charlie, she knew, would never have been reluctant.

Her sympathy was more with Lawton. Claire, evidently, had no such feeling. She had returned home with the express intention of catching her husband in flagrante, and any indignation she might have felt at his infidelity was more than offset by the malicious satisfaction of success.

"Get out of my bed, you trollop!" she screamed. "How dare you bring your fancy strumpets into my house Lawton, you—

you—filthy fornicator! And you had the impudence to accuse me of having something going on the side! I knew something like this was going on. I wonder if you have the nerve to face your friends after this. I know I shan't. And to think your secretary had to see you in these degrading circumstances."

She turned to Linda. "I'm sorry, Miss Saunders," she said, tearful with rage. "I thought it must be you he was misbehaving with. I don't know how you can go on working for him after this, knowing what kind of man he is. I hope you won't mind my attorney getting in touch with you as a witness to this depravity?"

She turned back to the bed, where the two bodies were still having some difficulty disentangling themselves.

"Lawton, I'm getting a divorce. I'm not living in this house with you another day. And get that floozy out of the house. I don't care whether she gets her clothes on or not, but get her out of here." She stormed out of the room, stopped, and her voice came from the hall. "I'm taking the car, you'll have to take taxis from now on or get yourself another car. Come along, Miss Saunders. You have your car, do you?"

"Thank you, Mrs. Wainright," Linda said. "I'll follow you out. But there are some things I must talk to Doctor Wainright about. You go ahead."

She watched Claire to the front door, and when it had slammed she turned once more into the bedroom and gazed with interest at the man she loved. For the first time she was looking at Lawton as he really was, the real Lawton, with his own face, not the Lawton in Charlie's body. With his own body, too, none of it left to the imagination. It was a strange sensation, like meeting a pen pal for the first time. He was younger looking than she expected, though there was strain in his face, probably from the past few days. Not quite as sexy looking as Charlie had seemed in the first flush of their relationship, but attractive in a less flashy way. And yet, surprisingly like Charlie, really. Did she have to fall in love all over again with this new man? she wondered.

"So you're Miss Saunders?" said the lady on the bed, standing up unself-consciously and gathering her scattered clothes. "That's an interesting development. Who does that make me, Miss Gwynn?"

"God forbid!" said Lawton with feeling, and sat up on the edge of the bed. "Let's not turn this fiasco into a horror story. Linda, it was Charlie, you know it was Charlie, don't you? I only just . . ." He stopped, remembering Miss Saunders.

"I know," she said. "Not to worry. May I sit down? I can't go on staring at you two like a tourist at a sex show. How about some introductions? I assume you two know each other? I'm Linda McClusky. I can't think why Mrs. Wainright mistook me for Miss Saunders."

"Hi, I'm Sam Saunders. Sam, short for Samantha. I think I'd better go and make myself look a bit more presentable, my hair must be a mess. You never know who may drop in. Have you been here long, by the way? The first I knew about having an audience was when my backside caught fire."

"We'd just arrived," Linda said. "Claire wasn't about to let the festivities go on any longer than she could help. I must say, though, it was quite an impressive exhibition. A Navy boy-friend I used to have told me they call that sort of thing an 'exibeesh' in Port Said."

"Glad you enjoyed it. We'll send out invitations next time." Miss Saunders left to look for the bathroom.

"There isn't going to be a next time if I have anything to do with it," Lawton said firmly as he stood up and reached for his clothes. "Linda, you do believe me, don't you? I only just arrived, right in the middle of it all."

"Yes darling, yes, it's alright, don't worry. But this is what I meant, we're never going to be sure when it's going to happen. Hey! You don't have to put on those pants on my account."

"Miss Saunders doesn't know about us," Lawton said. "I don't think she should know I'm . . ."

"Playing around?" Linda completed for him. "I'd say she's learned a few things about you tonight she didn't know before.

Well, aren't you going to kiss me now that I'm here, or are you too pooped to pucker? This is going to be my first kiss with the real you, you know that, don't you?"

Lawton hurriedly buttoned his shirt. "Darling, I'm so confused. I didn't expect ever to see you again."

"I said it wouldn't work. And it won't. But you are pleased to see me, aren't you?" Lawton put his arms about her and showed his pleasure. While they stood there holding each other, she told him how she decided she had to find out for sure, had to know whether she was in love with a Lawton who really did exist or whether she was going crazy. They were still embracing when Miss Saunders came back into the room, smiling brightly. For a woman so recently caught in the act by an irate wife, Linda thought, she looks remarkably cool. Wish I could get my hair to look like that so soon after climbing out of bed.

"Sam," she said, "you must think I'm dreadful, busting in on you two like that. I really should have been minding my own business, I suppose, but when Claire stormed in with steam coming out of her ears I just couldn't resist. Like following the fire truck."

Miss Saunders sat demurely on the edge of the bed. "I didn't know which of you was which at first. You were the first one I saw, so I thought you must be Mrs. Wainright. Until she started yelling."

Lawton reached out and took her hand. "This has been rotten for you," he said. "I'm terribly sorry. I should never have brought you home and risked something like this happening. I seem to be doing a lot of silly things lately."

"I wouldn't say it's been rotten at all." Miss Saunders giggled. "The first part was just great. But why did your wife come back? I thought she was supposed to be away for a few days."

"I guess she wanted to catch me out. We both accused each other of cheating this morning."

"Will she really divorce you?"

"Not on your account, Sam," Linda interrupted. "She doesn't know who you are, she thinks I'm you, she thinks she's going to use me as a witness but she doesn't know where to find me, so she's fresh out of luck on all counts."

"I'm afraid it's just about come to divorce, though,"

Lawton said. "Life has been impossible at home lately. Sam, you'll have to excuse my behavior in the office. Half the time I don't seem to know what I'm doing. And I can't apologize enough for what's happened tonight."

"It wasn't your fault. I guess a girl should look out for trouble when she sets out to seduce her boss. But you are the yummiest boss, you know. Isn't he?" She turned to Linda.

"Oh, he's yummy alright," agreed Linda. "But I'm not sure it's a good thing to let him know."

Miss Saunders got up from the bed. "It was lovely while it lasted. I can stop fantasizing about you now, and concentrate on the job." She put one arm round Lawton's neck and reached up to kiss him. "See you in the office. Nice meeting you, Linda. He really was hard to hook, and now I know why."

Linda went to the front door with her and stood watching while she drove away. When she got back to the bedroom Lawton was sitting on the bed with his head in his hands. She sat down beside him. "Is it so very bad?" she asked quietly.

"Couldn't be much worse," he said. "I couldn't take it this morning when you said you weren't coming back. But I know what you mean now. This sort of thing will keep happening. My life isn't my own any more. I'm surprised he's not breathing down my neck right now, telling me what to do, what to say, making me say things I don't intend to say."

"I shouldn't have been so rough on you," she said gently. "I'd been struggling with it all night, and I finally decided for my own sanity we had to make a break. I didn't want to. I didn't want to have to tell you. The only way I could do it was to be really hard, and that hurt you didn't it?"

"I suppose you were right, though. You have your own life to live without hanging about waiting for me to turn into a pumpkin every few hours." His face lit up. "Hey, now it's all over with Claire you can move in with me. Not into this house maybe, but we can live together."

"You still don't get it, do you?" she said patiently. "If we live together, then part of the time Charlie's going to be there in your place. When you change with Charlie you really become Charlie. And it's not Charlie I'm in love with, it's Lawton. When you're Charlie anything can happen. Sometimes you're like you and then suddenly you can become really rotten. Darling, can't you see I've got as much of a problem as you have? You're expecting me to love two men equally. You don't even look the same. Do you realize this is the first time I've ever seen your real face?"

She took his face between her two hands and looked into his eyes. "I was wrong this morning. Running away from it won't make it any better. We've both got problems, and if we don't help each other I can see us both heading for the booby hatch. We'll work something out."

She reached out a hand and started to unbutton his shirt. "Right now we should be able to reckon on a few hours to ourselves before another Change. With luck. I'd say you've had more than your fair share of being seduced in the last few days. How about you taking the initiative for once?"

CHAPTER 16

Whichever of the fates controlled The Changes was kind to them that night. It was a calculated risk on Linda's part. If she should wake up and find herself in bed with Charlie, any sort of unpleasantness could develop. But they were not disturbed. For once Charlie was not even intruding into Lawton's mind.

"He's got too much on his own mind at the moment," Lawton explained the next morning. "He's been fired from the club. And he's hitting the bottle again."

"Don't be too hard on him," Linda said. "His life's been upset, too. In his mind he's the one who's suffering and you're the also-ran."

"I suppose so," Lawton agreed reluctantly. "But he's the one who's making a mess of my life. It's as if he's deliberately setting out to wreck every situation he comes across."

"You haven't done so well with his, you know."

"God, Linda, where's all this going to end? It gets worse every day. When did it start? Sunday? I don't even know what day it is today, but it can't be more than a week, and everything's in ruins already."

"It's Saturday. This is the seventh day."

"Yesterday when you hung up on me I was ready to kill myself. Only I didn't know how."

"Darling, I'm sorry I did that. I guess I was trying to walk away from it, and we can't do that. But suicide's certainly not the way to go. You're not to think of suicide ever again. Do you understand that?"

"I guess so. But I don't see how I can go on like this if you're going to walk out on me."

"I'm not going to walk out on you. Now listen. This is a bad time for all three of us and we're going to have to work it out together, not run away from it. So I want you to promise me you'll keep fighting it and don't under any circumstances think about suicide. Is that a promise?"

"I guess so."

"Not 'I guess so.' I want a definite 'Yes.' I want a man, not a mouse. Do you promise?"

"Yes darling, yes, I promise," he said, smiling at her intensity. "If you're going to help me."

"Of course I'll help you, my darling, if we can find a way. But I can't move back into Charlie's apartment, and I can't move in with you, you understand that, don't you? I've got to find a way of getting you by yourself, uninterrupted. And now that I've found you as you really are I don't want any substitutes. I want you pure and unadulterated."

"Pure you've got." The pep talk had put some spirit into him. "As for adulteration, that's what you do to food when you stick strange things into it."

Linda began to laugh. "If you're going to get technical, that sounds more like what you've been doing to me."

"Miss McClusky," he protested, pretending to be shocked. "You seem to have the ability to drag even love down to a four letter level."

"Love's a four letter word already, dear. And I love you, so don't worry, I'm going to stick with you till we get this worked out. And after. I'll call you when I get home, and we'll see what the situation is then. You'll be here?"

"Where else? It's getting so I'm scared about what's going to happen next. I just want to stay on familiar ground. You must go to the office today, I suppose?"

"Got to make up for the time I've missed. I'll call you, darling. 'Bye."

Left to himself, alone, really alone for the first time since his marriage, Lawton found himself wallowing again in a slough of despair. The house was no longer home. Even Claire, uncongenial as she was, had been company. He could see no way to be alone with Linda, to be free of Chesney's influence, either after a Change or at times like this when Chesney might interject his own personality at any moment.

As if to emphasize the point, the intrusions began almost as soon as the thought had formed. All very well promising not to think about suicide, Chesney said. What other way out is there?

The voice was so real that he answered it aloud. "I've always despised suicides."

Looked a bit different yesterday, though, didn't it? What's to despise when there's nothing else?

There must be something else. This can't go on forever.

Why not? The loony bins are full of psychos hearing voices. Maybe something like this is what's put them there.

You mean I'm going crazy?

No. I mean maybe the crazies really aren't. Maybe they're really hearing voices, and no one believes them?

I've often wondered about that, he mused. You mean I could be locked up, too?

Why not? Society doesn't like people who act different.

Charlie left him alone with his depression after that. As usual his thoughts turned back to Linda. She was right. There was no way they could live together, or even spend much time together, till they could be sure Chesney wouldn't invade their privacy. Perhaps he was doing the same to Chesney? But he wasn't doing it consciously, so whatever he was doing to Chesney could only be a product of his own sub-conscious. And he'd never wished ill to anyone, so whatever he was doing or saying couldn't have any malice in it, surely? But each day seemed to bring some frightful new development. Already Chesney seemed to be sharing his mind. What next? Would he get to look more like Chesney? Would they finish up as two identical people? Or one, even?

He rushed into the bathroom to look in the mirror. There was no horror like the horror of that first morning, but certainly his face was more full, the lips more fleshy, and the eyes more puffy. What had he thought about that alien face the first time it had stared back at him out of Chesney's mirror? Well used, he had thought. That was the way his own face was beginning to look. And it was only a week! In another week what would he look like? Where would he be? In a mental institution?

He ran out of the bathroom to the phone. He must talk to Linda. To someone, but preferably Linda. If he wasn't crazy already he would be after another day alone like this. He picked up the phone.

Better not, said the voice. What are we going to tell her? We're cracking up? We're a mouse after all?

She understands. She promised to help.

Like she did yesterday? She hung up yesterday. She left us to it.

But she came back.

She'll hang up again. She won't want to be tied up with a crazy. She wants to keep us at arm's length.

Only because of you. If you'd learn to control yourself we wouldn't be so badly off. And keep out of my mind.

Can't stop the tide running, Lawton Baby. We're one and the same now. I've got it figured out. We'll finish up as a double identity. Dual personality if you like. And the stronger one gets to call the shots.

But that's madness.

Too true. Very undignified for the Curator of the Museum. Carted away, kicking and screaming. The other way's cleaner.

What other way?

Suicide. That way we get to make the decision. To be, or not to be, that's the decision.

But that's worse than going mad.

Is it? Worse than being shut away for a lifetime? It's quick, very easy.

Maybe it's easy for you. I wouldn't know how to go about it.

Bullet in the brain, that's all. Instantaneous.

I haven't got a gun.

Oh yes we have. Leave it to Chesney.

The more he thought about it, the more it seemed to make sense, and the less repugnant the idea of suicide seemed. One quick decision and all their problems would be solved. His, Chesney's and Linda's. And the gun was there, of course, at the back of the top drawer of the desk at Park Plaza. He had forgotten about it, it had been there so long. He could get it next time they changed.

The very possibility of bringing the whole sequence of horror to an end, whatever the end, whatever the method, seemed to lift a great weight from him. It was in an almost euphoric mood that he phoned Linda at five o'clock. "How was the day?" he asked.

"Fine, thanks, even though it was a Saturday. Wonderful how much you can get done when there's no one else around and the phone doesn't ring. How was your day?"

"Started badly, but it's better now." No need to tell her why. "Take you out to dinner tonight?"

There was a silence at the other end. "Lawton dear, We've got to set some ground rules for how we're going to carry on. That way we both know where we stand."

He said she'd hang up again, Lawton thought, deflated. She's backing away again.

"If we try to rush into each others' arms every moment of the day we're going to run headlong into Changes and all sorts of grief. We're going to need some self-discipline, darling, and just get together when we have a good chance of being undisturbed. Even then there's always a risk."

He said nothing.

"Does that make sense, darling? It's been nearly twenty-four hours now, hasn't it? It's almost bound to happen again soon. We're going to have to ration ourselves to the times when the odds aren't against us."

"So it's No for tonight?" There was a hard edge to his voice.

"Don't be like that, darling. If you want me to survive this thing without a breakdown you've got to understand. Do you understand? Lawton?"

But this time it was he who hung up. The sooner it came the better. The sooner he could get at the gun the sooner it would be all over. He went to bed early, and wept quietly for the Lawton who might have been, the career that might have been, the marriage that might have been, the love affair that nearly was.

His sleep was filled with nightmares. Little remained in his memory but jumbled fragments by morning, but one incident was so clearly etched that it stayed to haunt him long into the day. A face was leering out at him from that mirror he would never forget, the one in Charlie Chesney's bathroom where he had first caught sight of Chesney's bloodshot eyes. It was a dreadful face, with drooling mouth and vacant eyes. It was his own face, he knew. It must be, because it was his own reflection and the mirror couldn't lie. And yet it was an alien face, beckoning, enticing him to join it in that other world inside the looking glass, an insane world where everything was back to front and impossibility was the norm. He screamed and fought against the power that seemed to draw him in, but all the strength had left his limbs and he found himself pulled inexorably through into the madness on the other side. And then, the worst of all, he found himself becoming one with that obscenity with the gibbering face, and he knew that he was trapped for ever on the inside looking out.

Damp with sweat, and shaking with the memory of his own demented face, he went to the phone with some vague idea of making his apologies for hanging up on Linda the night before.

"Where are you, Baby?" Linda cut in urgently as soon as she heard his voice. "It hasn't happened yet? Listen darling. I've been talking to a friend. He's a psychiatrist at the University. He wants to talk to you. It's Sunday, but he's at home this morning."

"That's just great!" Lawton exploded. "You think I'm crazy. You're trying to get me put away."

"Lawton, listen. People go to psychiatrists for help. Millions of people tell you they see their shrink regularly, and no one calls them crazy. I called him up first because I thought he might be able to help me. It's just that he may be able to help us both, show us how to cope with this thing without cracking up."

"Suppose he won't believe me? Suppose he wants to put me away?"

"Lawton dear, stop and think for a minute. He's a research scientist at the University. He's interested in the paranormal. He wants to know more about you, not put you away. He's prepared to give up his Sunday morning to see if he can help, that's all."

"Will you come with me?"

"Of course, darling. I'll call him and tell him we're coming."

"Shall I pick you up at your place?"

She laughed. "You're forgetting something. Claire took your car. I'll be right over to pick you up."

Alexander Wronski was a quiet-spoken man in his middle forties, with a ready smile under a heavy mustache. Lawton was prepared to be treated like a specimen under a microscope, but beyond an initial calculating scrutiny from steady wide-set eyes as they shook hands, Wronsky's manner was hospitable and warm.

"Sorry about the mess," he apologized as he cleared books off the chairs. "This is my study and no-one else usually comes in here, not even my wife. Can I get you a drink?"

At ten in the morning? thought Lawton. He's testing me.

After the social preliminaries, Linda excused herself to wait in the day room. Thrown to the wolves, thought Lawton. Now I get torn to pieces.

"Linda tells me you're interested in the Fifteenth Dynasty?" Wronski said.

"Well, yes." Lawton was unprepared for this.

"I always understood there was so little known about that period. They didn't leave much behind, did they?"

"That's the popular conception," Lawton agreed. "Or rather that's the conception we've inherited from some of the earlier historians.

But in fact we have a lot of very graphic descriptions of important events and about their way of life. And far from there being a dearth of artifacts of the period, we've been unearthing Egyptian pottery and jewelry and ornaments and clay tablets and scarabs in practically every country of the world as it was known at that time. They clearly had a flourishing foreign trade."

So, within fifteen minutes, it was a more relaxed Lawton Wainright who outlined the incidents of the past week, from the initial ghastly discovery in Charlie Chesney's bedroom to Chesney's more recent intrusions into his mind. One detail he carefully left out of the narrative was the discussion of suicide. That was an option he wanted to keep open.

"You say you seriously considered the possibility of these Changes being fantasies in your own mind?" Wronski asked.

"That's what I thought it must be at first. After all, what rational person would believe he was really changing personalities with another man?"

"But you believe it now?"

"It's not a question of belief any more. It's actually happening, and other people are getting caught up in it."

"Yes. Well. These Changes, now. Apart from the initial one, and the Change back again, they all seem to have happened in connection with some sexual episode. Does that strike you as significant?"

Lawton saw a ray of hope. "And three of them were with Miss Saunders and Miss Gwynn! You mean they're being triggered by sex?"

Alex Wronski smiled tolerantly. "That's one possible interpretation, certainly. But can you think of another?"

Lawton thought. "Not really."

"Never mind."

"But that certainly figures," Lawton said eagerly. "It's been a day and a night since the last Change, that's the longest yet. And I haven't seen a woman in that time. Apart from Linda this morning.

475-ALLE

Do you think I can stop them happening if I keep away from Miss Saunders and Miss Gwynn?"

"What do you think?"

"It seems like a good possibility. But why should that cause the Changes?"

"That's a good question. Here's another question. Do you think you'd be able to keep away from them?"

"Well, I'd have to transfer Miss Saunders to another office . . ."

"I mean, do you want to keep away from them?"

"Of course! It was Chesney who couldn't keep his hands off them. They don't mean anything to me."

"But you seem to have been very greatly impressed by Miss Saunders' nipples and Miss Gwynn's bust."

"You're not suggesting I've got a fixation on breasts?"

"They did figure rather importantly in your story just now, didn't they? How long is it since you had sex with your wife? Apart from the other night after you found her locked in the bathroom?"

"Must be several months," Lawton said. "But what's that got to do with it? You think all this is hallucination because I'm not—er—having sex regularly? I've already explained how it can't be imagination." He was becoming angry. "I can prove it quite easily. Phone up Chesney. He'll tell you it's happening to him too."

Not on your Aunt Nelly, he won't, Chesney's voice broke in, as if he had been listening all along. No way I'm getting mixed up with a shrink.

You wouldn't let me down like that, Lawton thought. I've got to convince him.

What's it matter what he thinks? That's not going to solve our problem. There's only one sure way out.

"You really want me to check with Mr. Chesney?" Wronski asked. "What if he says he doesn't know you?"

"He will," Lawton said miserably. "He's talking to me now. He says he'll deny it."

"Why do you think he'd do that, if he's suffering from these Changes too?"

"He doesn't want anything to do with you. He's scared of being put away. He says the only way out is to get rid of one of us."

"Which one?"

"Me."

"Charlie Chesney is trying to persuade you to kill yourself?"

Lawton put his head in his hands. He had let out his secret. Now they wouldn't give him the chance even to kill himself.

"Are you scared of being put away, as you call it?"

Lawton nodded. Chesney's intervention had destroyed all hope that Wronski might help him.

"How long have you known Charlie Chesney?" Wronski asked.

"I've never met him. Not face to face."

"But you thought he might be having an affair with your wife?"

"Not really. That was just something he said to bug her."

"And your wife had never had anything to do with Chesney?"

"Of course not."

"But you think she has been having an affair with someone? Perhaps I should talk to Chesney?" Wronski was watching Lawton's reaction closely. "He might not deny changing places with you, and if he does we're really no worse off, are we?"

"Which means you don't believe me," Lawton said bitterly.

Wronski looked up the number in the book and dialed deliberately, watching Lawton.

"Good morning. Mister Chesney? I'm a friend of Lawton Wainright. Lawton Wainright. You don't? You're quite sure you don't know him? Doctor Lawton Wainright. Well, I'm sorry to have troubled you, Mister Chesney, and thank you. Goodbye."

"He's lying!" Lawton cried out. "He doesn't want to get involved with you." He felt sick with disappointment. And fear. If Chesney was going to deny him what hope was there of ever proving he was not imagining everything? Faintness threatened to engulf him. Wronski's face became a blur. The room began to move, and he was spinning round and round.

So it was happening again? This time there had been no voice to warn of the Change, no sound except the pounding of his own pulse.

Then it was past. He was standing beside Chesney's telephone with the echo of his own voice in his ears. "Who? Lawton Wainright? Don't know him. Sure I'm sure. No trouble. Goodbye."

The echo of his own betrayal! And to compound the calumny, that Judas was no doubt playing the fool and destroying every vestige of his credibility with Professor Wronski. He had never found anything in Charlie Chesney's personality to admire, but up till now there had been nothing to suggest the depths of treachery the man was capable of. Suddenly, the whole perfidious plot became clear. The constant persuasion that all his problems could be solved by suicide. The warnings of insanity, of being shut away for life. And now the final denial, calculated to prove his paranoia. The closer Chesney could drive him to the threat of incarceration, the more likely he would be to kill himself. And only with Lawton out of the way could Chesney see any hope of release from a lifetime of Changes.

How blind he had been! He should have seen all this before. And yet he hadn't been aware of it in Chesney's mind the last time they had changed. The idea must have germinated since last time. Germinated? That was for healthy things. Putrefied was closer to the mark!

Surely there was something he could do? He could call back. With Chesney's voice, from Chesney's phone. Confirm the whole of Chesney's involvement in The Changes. Tell Wronski that he was just as near to cracking up under the strain as Lawton was. Vindicate himself, and get back at Chesney at the same time. He grabbed the phone book and riffled through the pages with clumsy, impatient fingers.

Wroclawski, Wrona, Wronna, Wroolie, Wrople. No Wronski! Dear god, not again! Not another nail in the coffin! I can't have imagined the whole interview? Linda was there. It must have happened. Or was it all just another nightmare like the hideous leering face? My whole life lately seems to alternate so fast between short periods of hope and hours of despair.

He put down the phone book. A spark of reason flashed across the darkness closing in on him. The phone book. The phone! I must have answered the phone or I wouldn't be standing here now, beside the phone. Wronski must have called, and I didn't dream him up. His number's not in the book because—he doesn't want it in the book. It's an unlisted number. Relief flooded in. I'm beginning to doubt myself all the time now. Have to get a better grip on myself if I'm to beat that bastard at his own game.

But relief was short lived. His one chance of proving Chesney was lying rested in that telephone number, and the number wasn't in the book. Call his office and ask for his private number. On a Sunday? Drive to his home and confront Chesney in front of him. But he hadn't a clue where Wronski lived, hadn't been paying attention while Linda drove him there. Look up his address in a street directory. Where? Library. On a Sunday morning? He sank into the armchair, beaten at every turn. What the hell did it matter anyway? Chesney was right, there was only one way out.

He got up out of the chair and went to the desk. Top drawer. At the very back. The gun was there all right. The sight of a gun made him nervous. He knew nothing at all about guns. He knew there was a safety catch, because he'd read about it somewhere. He took the gun out of the drawer, and surprised himself by opening it confidently and checking the ammunition, then snapping back the safety catch and putting it away in an inside pocket. It made an ugly bulge, but he only had to get to the parking lot. The Wainright house would be locked. The side door to the garage was always open, he remembered. The gun would be safe enough tucked away on the top shelf above the battery charger, and Wainright would know where to find it when he needed it.

And need it he certainly would. Cheerful Charlie Chesney would have to see to that if Charlie Chesney was somehow to remain cheerful. The situation was already intolerable, and it had to be resolved speedily. What did Hitler call it? The Final Solution?

He was inclined to leave right away, to be sure of getting to Croftdown Road before Wainright got back from the shrink.

He had no wish to meet himself face to face. The thought repelled him, frightened him almost. And yet he ought to stay by the phone until lunchtime in case Marvin called. He dare not miss the offer of a job. It wasn't so much the loss of income that mattered. He just had to get back to work right away and show the world they couldn't keep Charlie Chesney down. But Marvin was probably out playing golf. Marvin didn't normally let loyalty to his clients spoil his weekends.

He sat down again, considering how best to make sure Wainright used the gun without delay. He wouldn't need much more pushing, he was already on the brink. He must know the trickcyclist couldn't possibly believe his story. Persuade him Wronski would have him committed, play on his horror of the loony-bin. A few anonymous phone calls might help. Convince him he was going nuts. Persecution mania, wasn't it? And if Wainright was still too chicken to use the gun, he would have to do the job himself. Make it look like suicide. The shrink would testify the man was obviously suicidal.

CHAPTER 17

A little more than three and a half miles away, Professor Alex Wronski had not been particularly surprised to observe a change in the demeanor of the man he was interviewing. He had intentionally indicated by his questioning that there might be some psychological reason for the phenomena that Lawton was insisting were real. Goading him, in fact, to some reaction that might be revealing. After the phone call, which seemed to refute Lawton's assertion that Charlie Chesney was also involved in the Changes, Wronski noted with satisfaction that there was indeed a new reaction.

"I guess that kind of looks like the old imagination must be working overtime, eh Doc?" Charlie said, grinning sheepishly.

"So you don't think he's lying, then?" prompted Wronski.

"I guess not."

"You expected him to say he didn't know you?"

"Well, this voice was telling me he would, wasn't it?"

"Which voice?"

"Chesney's voice. I told you. He talks to me a lot. He's the one who puts the sexy ideas in my head."

"About Miss Saunders' breasts?"

"Tits," corrected Charlie. "Other women have breasts. Sam's are tits. Rosemary's are boobs."

"You seem to be quite a connoisseur. Have you had this interest long?"

"All my life. Ever since I got tired of elephants."

"Elephants' breasts?"

"Elephants don't have breasts. They have trunks."

Professor Wronski felt it was time to try a different tack. "Does this voice put other ideas into your head?"

Now's the time to prepare the ground, thought Charlie. "Only sex and suicide. He's trying to get rid of me."

"Does he say he is?"

"No, but I know he is. Same as I know you want to put me away."

"Why do you think I should want to put you away?"

"That's what trickcyclists are for, isn't it?"

"Psychiatrists?"

"Same difference."

Wronski looked at his watch. "Why do you think he wants to get rid of you?"

"He wants my secretary."

"Why?"

"Cheeze, Doc, I guess you haven't seen my secretary."

"And what about Miss Gwynn?"

"She's got a secretary of her own."

Professor Wronski breathed deeply. "One last question, Doctor Wainright. Have you ever tried to commit suicide?"

"Sure Doc," Charlie said ruefully. "Three nights ago in front of a whole house full of people."

"You weren't hurt?"

"Couple of bruises when I fell off the stool, is all."

* * *

Sunlight streamed into the kitchen of the Park Plaza apartment where Lawton was putting ice into his second gin and tonic. This is a woman's kitchen, he thought. Who needs a window in the kitchen unless they're going to spend all day there? He thought regretfully of Linda, who seemed to find her way about the kitchen from the moment she walked in. She was good to have about the place, helped me through those first grizzly days. What was it made me throw her out? Another one of those fits when I seem to lose control and do stupid things. Jealousy, too, I guess. She's so obviously in love with that wimp. Then she got so damned uppity.

Once a woman wants to be the boss that's the beginning of the end. If I hadn't thrown her out that night it would have happened some other time.

When the phone rang, he put down the glass and hurried into the other room. It had to be Marvin. About bloody time, too. "Chesney," he said.

"Lawton?" asked Linda's voice tentatively.

"No it's not bloody Lawton," he snarled. "What do you want?"

"You don't sound very friendly," she said.

"I don't feel very friendly. I was expecting Marvin. I've been waiting in all morning, and it pisses me off."

I've got to get through to Lawton somehow, Linda thought. How do I shake him out? Some kind of shock?

"Claire's at the house," she said. "She's stripping the place. Taking away everything that's worth anything. She threw your clothes out onto the front lawn, and she's banged up the front of the car."

"So she's banged up the car! She needs Lawton to bang her up. I'm pretty sure she's getting it on the side, anyway."

"Lawton!" Linda shouted. "Lawton, snap out of it. I've got to talk to you. Tell Charlie to get off the line. Lawton! Lawton! Lawton! Do you hear me?"

"Yes darling, yes," laughed Lawton. "Receiving you loud and clear. What's all the panic?"

"Oh darling, I was afraid I wouldn't be able to get through to you."

"You were on the wrong channel, that's all. Are you alright?"

"Yes, I'm fine. Did you hoist in what I said about Claire at the house?"

"It's been her house ever since we moved in. There's not much of mine there. As long as she doesn't take my old letter sweater."

"That's not really what I called about." Linda's voice was calmer. "I talked to Alex. Alex Wronski. He said he's concerned about you thinking about suicide. Darling, you promised me you'd stop thinking about it."

"I know," Lawton said. "It wasn't my idea. Chesney keeps talking to me about it, trying to persuade me."

"Darling, that's awful! I can't believe Charlie's like that. Are you sure it's really him?"

"Yes, it's not just paranoia. I found out today. He forgot we both know what's in each other's mind. He's trying to make me so scared of going round the bend I'll be ready to kill myself."

"But why on earth? He hasn't any reason to hate you that much."

"He doesn't. He just despises me. But he figures if one of us is gone there can't be any more Changes."

"If that's the case, why shouldn't he be the one?"

"He's got the gun. He's going to take it to Croftdown Road for me to use. He's going to keep working on me, and phoning me, till I break down and do it."

"Well you're jolly well not going to break down and do it. You don't want to do it, do you?"

"I don't know. I really don't know. I keep thinking I must be going crazy. I know Wronski thinks so. I don't want to spend the rest of my life shut away."

"Darling, he doesn't think that, I'm sure. You mustn't be that way."

"Anyway, that's not all. If he can't persuade me to do it he's going to come after me with the gun and do it himself."

"That's terrible! We've got to do something. Can we go to the police?"

Lawton laughed. "With what? Tell them a well known comedian's trying to kill a man he's never met?"

"I'm frightened. I didn't know he could be like that.

Do you want me to come and be there with you?"

"You know I'd love you to come," he said. "But you heard what he was like on the phone to you just now. I don't think there's any danger while I'm here. He's not going to do anything to hurt Charlie Chesney. And he wants to make it look like suicide."

"We've got to figure out some way of keeping him away from you. Can't you get rid of the gun while you're there?"

"That's it! Now you're really thinking, darling," he exclaimed. "It's in my pocket now. I'll throw it down the garbage chute as soon as I hang up."

"No, do it now, quickly. And then come back to the phone."

She heard him put down the phone. A moment later it was picked up again. "Nice try, Linda Baby," Charlie said silkily. "He wasn't quick enough."

The phone went dead.

* * *

Only eight days before, a little more than a week that had proved to be the longest in Lawton Wainright's life, waking to the magazine cut-outs and the pale blue scalloped drapes and satin headboards had meant return to the security of home. This morning, as he opened his eyes and knew that he was back in Croftdown Road, it neither seemed like home nor was there any feeling of security. Instead he woke to overhanging fear. A fear not so much of death itself—that was something he had been prepared to welcome yesterday—but the dread of being hunted down, of waiting, never knowing when the blow might fall. He had been safer back in Chesney's apartment, sharing bed and board and body with his executioner. There had been no way Chesney could hurt him without hurting himself. Today it was open season on Wainright.

Chesney still had the gun. Now that he knew Lawton was aware of what he planned, he was not likely to make a present of the gun on the off chance Lawton might use it on himself. And Chesney must be in a hurry. Every day's delay presumably brought him closer to that same state of mental collapse that threatened all three of them. So it could happen at any time. Chesney could be on his way at this very minute.

Lawton flung off the bedclothes and ran to the window, not knowing why, not knowing what he expected to see out there.

Chesney's car? Chesney standing in the garden waiting for him? Get a grip on yourself. This is not a gangland execution. It won't be a bullet through the window from a speeding car. This has got to look like suicide. He has to get close.

He still had time to get out of the house. He could go to Linda's apartment. But Chesney would think of looking there. Was Chesney able to read his mind, know where he was, what he was doing, what he was thinking? It seemed unlikely, because he had no clue what Chesney was up to. That was a development that might happen at any time, though. One danger was that Chesney could still enter his mind and influence his thoughts. Could he keep him out if he were strong willed enough? Could he match the strength of Chesney's personality? Could he and Linda together keep him out? So where was he to go? Somewhere Chesney wouldn't know or couldn't get to. And yet he couldn't stay away from work forever. He could keep the house locked, but he couldn't keep Chesney out of the museum.

The first move was to phone Linda. It was only a little after six o'clock, but she would be concerned about him. She might have some ideas.

"I'm back," he announced when she came sleepily to the phone. "Linda, he's after me. I've got to get out of this house. Somewhere he can't find me."

"Darling," she said firmly, sensing his rising panic, "the most important thing is you mustn't lose your cool."

"I know, Linda, but I'm scared. You don't know what it's like. I only just woke up and he could have got into the house while I was asleep. He could be here now."

"He could have killed you by now in that case," she replied practically.

"Well, he could be here any time."

"Alright, why don't you get out of the house right away?"

"I'm not dressed yet."

"Alright then as soon as you're dressed. If he wants to make it look like suicide he can't do it while you're with other people.

Out in the street, or in a taxi or in a store. So get outside the house, and call me from a pay phone. A gas station or somewhere. He can't touch you there. And you may even be able to give him the slip if you hurry, and he won't know where you are till the next Change."

"I'm not sure about that. But I guess I panicked a bit. How long are you going to be there?"

"I'm going to call in sick again, so I'll be here till you call. There's something important we need to talk about. Have you got any appointments today?"

"I've got to meet with the Board this morning. I can't possibly miss that."

"Oh for heaven's sake, Lawton, if you had the flu or got run over by a bus they'd have to do without you! Anyway, we'll talk about that later. Hang up now, and get out as quickly as you can. I'll wait here."

He checked the back door and the door to the garage to make sure they were locked. And then it took all the courage he had, but he crept out to the garage to lock the side door and disconnect the electric door. He dressed quickly, choosing something just barely formal enough for the Board meeting. There was no time to shave, so he gathered up his electric shaver and lotion and toothpaste and toothbrush and a towel and put them in his briefcase. Linda would be proud of me, he thought. No panic. Got to think clearly. He left by the back door, walking quickly through the garden and wondering if there was any point in paying the gardener any longer for twice weekly visits. At the bottom of the garden, a small gate gave onto the back lane that ran parallel with Croftdown Road.

A sense of adventure was replacing the fear. He had never done anything like this before. All he need do, he decided, was think ahead, try to predict what Chesney's moves would be, and make sure he made no careless moves himself. But this was not a Boy Scout exercise. This was serious. As he walked quickly down the back lane, he thought of the neighbors, those of them who knew him. If any of them saw him now, would they believe for a moment that stuffy Lawton Wainright was fleeing for his life? He tried to put himself in Chesney's place. To drive up to the house, he would take the direct route from the main road. The only other way led all round the crescent. It made sense for Lawton to detour round the crescent and strike the main road beyond the turn-off Chesney would use, at the corner by the Chevron station.

There was a bank of four telephone booths at the edge of the gas station forecourt. No doors for privacy, but at least they were all unoccupied.

"So far so good," he said cheerfully when Linda answered.

"Where are you, darling?"

"Chevron station near the house. I don't think he can have seen me."

"He may not be anywhere near yet. He may wait till later and just work on your nerves. I know he's not doing any good to mine."

"We've got to talk. Now listen. The best place to meet is somewhere public, like a hotel lobby or a coffee shop. We may have lost him anyway, but if he finds us he can't do anything with people around."

"How about the Hilton?" he suggested.

"If we make it the Egmont coffee shop we can sit there as long as we like. It's near the Law Courts, so it's usually full of legal beagles talking shop. Alright?"

"Right. I'll phone for a . . ." He stopped.

"What is it? Are you alright?"

"It's his car," Lawton whispered, the awful realization making his voice crack. The adventure was gone. The dread was back as he watched the familiar red and black convertible pull in to the gas station.

"Charlie?"

"Yes." He turned away and hunched over the phone. "He's just driven up. He must be able to tell where I am." His hand was shaking so much that the mouthpiece hit his nose and brought the tears to his eyes.

"Maybe it's coincidence he's just stopped there. Is he getting gas?"

"No. He's parked. He's getting out. He's coming over here. Linda, I'm going to make a run for it."

"Try and get to the Egmont then," she shouted urgently. "I'll wait for you there."

But he had left it too late to run. Chesney was blocking his exit from the phone booth, hand reaching into his pocket. And yet he was not looking at Lawton. He was looking down at the handful of change he had pulled from his pocket. Then, miraculously, he went into the box next to Lawton and picked up the phone.

"Oh my god, Linda. He just came here to phone," Lawton whispered. "He hasn't even seen me." He began to giggle uncontrollably until the giggles turned to sobs. "I thought he was going to kill me then. He had his hand in his pocket. I thought he was reaching for . . ."

"Keep your head turned away," Linda ordered. "Don't look round at him whatever he does. Don't even peek. He mustn't see you. He's probably calling your house to see if you're home. Can you see his car without looking round at him?"

"Yes, I'm looking at it now."

"Good. Then keep your back to him and watch for him to get back into the car. Are you going to be alright?"

"Yes darling. I'm all right now. I thought this was all a lot of fun when I left the house, but it's turned into serious business. Why don't I phone for a taxi now while I'm waiting for him to go?"

"No don't do that," she said quickly. "Don't move or do anything that might make him look at you. And keep talking to me so I know you're alright till after he's gone."

"I think he's finished," Lawton whispered. "I think I heard his money coming back. That means he didn't get through."

"He wouldn't if he was calling you. Watch his car now, but keep your hand in front of your face."

"You must think me an awful wet Willie," he said. "I completely lost my nerve just now."

"So what are you supposed to do when you're expecting to be killed any moment? Don't you think I'd have had hysterics or passed out or something if that happened to me? People are only brave in books, darling. You were splendid."

"He's getting into the car. I think we're home free. Where do you think he'll go now?"

"He'll try here, probably. I'm leaving now. See you at the Egmont, right?"

CHAPTER 18

There were no more alarms. Lawton felt a moment of panic when Linda was not at the Egmont. But just as he found two vacant seats she came in through the entrance from the parking lot, trim and leggy in slacks and high heels, and smiling brightly as her eyes found him.

"Hi!" she greeted him. "I expect you could do with something stronger after that experience."

"You bet your pretty little tushy I could, Linda Baby," he replied coarsely. "Let's find some place with a license."

She looked at him sharply and the smile left her face. "This is something you've got to put a stop to," she said firmly. "There's no reason why you've got to put up with him butting in, darling. It's just a matter of who's got the stronger personality, and what I've seen of Charlie Chesney there's no strength there at all. It's just he's used to walking all over people and getting his own way."

"Damn right, Baby. Chesney always gets what he wants. And right now Chesney's in the mood for you." He reached across and grabbed Linda's wrist.

Without a word Linda swung her free hand across, and delivered a slap to Lawton's face that resounded across the room and turned every head toward them. Lawton's head was jerked back by the impact and his grip relaxed.

"We'll show you who gets what they want," she said through clenched teeth. "You couldn't get your pants on without a drink inside you, you alcoholic wimp. You take him Lawton."

"I'm not very experienced in the art of insulting," Lawton said quietly. "But frankly I don't think your personality could get you to first base in a second rate whorehouse unless you tanked up first.

There's something lacking in you, Chesney, and I'd say it's very nearly everything. All you've got going for you is bombast and a big mouth, and I shall be very much obliged if you'll kindly crawl back into your hole or I shall have to put you there."

Linda gave a shriek of laughter. "Beautiful!" she gasped. "So restrained. So very much to the point. And you say you've had no experience? I'm sorry about the slap, my darling—it's gone! There's no mark. Your face isn't even red any more."

"And it doesn't hurt any more. It was Chesney's, and I think he's taken it with him."

"Do you think he'll be even more vindictive now?"

"I don't think he's even conscious of butting in. I must be doing the same to him, but I'm not aware of it. Must be something in our subconscious. Now that I've told him off, maybe I'll be able to push him around more, wherever he is."

"Do you think you can persuade him not to come after you with the gun?"

"I'm probably trying, but it depends who stays in control. Perhaps while I'm in control here he's in control there. And vice versa."

"Lawton darling, you sound so much better. And that's what I had to talk to you about. Alex Wronski phoned again last night. He's very interested in you. He says he doesn't know what it's all about but he wants you to let him try some ideas on you."

Lawton waved a hand at her. "The point is, does he believe me, or does he think I'm imagining it?"

"That's all settled, darling. We both forgot something important. It's not just your word against Chesney's at all. I've been with you both. I've seen you both in your own homes. I've seen both your faces. I know you're two different people. And he knows I'm not making it up. He says paranormal experiences can be triggered by psychological upsets, like strain or marriage problems or all sorts of things. He thinks he may be able to stop it if he can remove the cause."

"Remove my marital problems? I should be so lucky!"

"Darling, I'm afraid you're being just a little bit self-centered. You're assuming this is your problem, and Charlie just happened to be the other person. Have you thought this might be all Charlie's problem, and you've got mixed up in it by accident?"

"You mean it might be Chesney's drink problem? Or sex?"

"It could be something like that. Anyway, Alex wants to try to help you both. Will you give it a try?"

Lawton shook his head doubtfully. "What do I have to do?"

"He wants you to spend a few days at University Hospital . . ."

"I told you he'd want to put me away," Lawton cut in. "No way is he going to get me in the nut house."

"Lawton, this isn't good enough. It's no good having a closed mind about this. We all need whatever help we can get, and I think you'd better start thinking about us as well as yourself. Even Charlie. It's not his fault any more than it's yours. And this paranoia about being put away is stupid. Alex has a research unit at the University. He wants to find out how to stop all this. He can't do it at home, can he, particularly if you're going to be hiding out."

She stopped. They looked at each other, each thinking the same thing.

"If I spend a few days under the microscope, Chesney won't be able to get at me," Lawton said slowly.

"You'd be so much under observation he wouldn't dare touch you. That might solve our problem."

"And you think Wronski may be able to find out what's triggering the Changes and put a stop to them?"

"He doesn't promise anything. But it's worth a try, isn't it?"

Lawton thought for a few moments. "I think that slap you gave me did me a lot of good. I'm not so scared now. Or at least I feel I've got the guts to face it."

"You had the guts all along, darling. Charlie was destroying your confidence in yourself, that's all. No more suicide?"

"Not now. Definitely not. I feel more like fighting now. You've shown me how. And it helps to know Wronski believes me. Let's give him a try."

"You phone him, then, and make the arrangements. Are you going to cancel the Board meeting?"

"Linda, it's more than ever important now that I don't miss it," he said seriously. "I've got to get leave of absence, for one thing. But more important, I've got to face Miss Gwynn. If you want me to keep fighting I can't run away from that."

"You're right. You're always right." She smiled at him with approval. "I must stop telling you what to do."

They drove back to Croftdown Road to collect the clothes and other things that Lawton would need. They took the precaution of approaching via the Crescent, and watching quietly from the car for a few minutes before parking in the back lane. Then they drove out to the University campus, and Linda left Lawton at Professor Wronski's office.

"I'm your chauffeur, not your mother," she quipped. "You don't need me hanging round."

"I guess I shall be able to get to a phone," he thought aloud. "I'll call you every evening."

"Unless you've changed again," she reminded him. "We've got to face that possibility."

All through Lawton Wainright's life since childhood, the approbation of other people, their approval of him as an individual, had been of great concern to him. Apart, then, from any determination to persuade Professor Wronski that the Changes were really taking place, he was concerned to impress him that Chesney's foolery was not a part of his own pattern of behavior, that he respected Wronski far more than to behave in that way.

Wronski, for his part, was more convinced of the reality of the Changes than Lawton realized. Charlie's denial had been of little importance once Linda confirmed that she had been a party to the whole episode. Wronski was concerned to discover the trigger for what he called the Paranormal Experiences.

"I want you to come and work with me as a partner, in effect," he explained. "First we have to determine whether these phenomena are the result of a form of mass hypnosis in which both Linda and you are persuaded to believe they are real. Certainly this doesn't seem likely, because you and Linda had no previous connection until the first episode. If we determine that some form of Paranormal Experience is occurring then we have to discover the cause, and remove it. But first let me assure you that the only form of paranoia I detect concerns your fear of being 'shut away' as you call it. There is no foundation for that fear."

"How long is this going to take?" Lawton wanted to know. "I have a job to do."

"I know that," Wronski said. "I can't even make an estimate of the time it may take to achieve success. But let us set ten days for an intensive observation and experimentation here. After that you can make your own decision based on what success we've had."

Lawton felt more relaxed than he had for days, particularly since the death threat was at least temporarily postponed. Relaxation therapy was to feature strongly in the early experiments to determine whether stress played any part as a trigger.

"I want you to do whatever you feel like doing," Wronski told him. "Within the area of the psychiatric wing. Read, write, watch television, talk to the patients or the staff. I want you as relaxed as it's possible to be away from your home environment."

"Home environment hasn't been particularly relaxed for quite a long time," Lawton observed. "If I give you a list of books I'd like from your library I shall be pretty content. How about exercise?"

"The grounds are quite extensive. There's a small lake, as you probably know, with a sort of mini bird sanctuary. You'll find that a very pleasant spot for reading. But I must ask you to check with the Nurse Supervisor before you go out, in case we need you for anything. Possibly you can come to some arrangement about a specific period each day?"

The Nurse Supervisor, wearing the nametag Sonia Bazett, proved to be a softly spoken woman with a toothy smile, grubby glasses and the remains of acne. Too softly spoken, Lawton thought. Sounds as if she's trying to soothe a baby. Or a psycho. Better than your average hospital nurse, though, who seems to feel she has to shout to get through to you. But that smile could certainly be switched on and off a lot more subtly. She's like an illustration from a textbook on How To Handle a Mental Patient.

Ms. Bazett came into his room as he was finishing unpacking his things. "We have a real treat for you, Doctor Wainright. You're not a medical doctor, are you? No. I was hoping not. They make terrible patients, you know. Now, we've got some therapy for you. I call it the Water Lily Treatment. It's a wonderfully relaxing bath of warm water, and you lie suspended in it with the water flowing all round you, and you just FLOAT ON THE SURFACE OF THE WATER LIKE A WATER LILY." The last sentence became a song, the smile became more toothy, and the glasses seemed to grow opaque like the bottoms of a pair of champagne bottles. And her right hand undulated across the air to demonstrate the joys of water lily life.

This lady's working in the right department, Lawton thought uncharitably. She won't have far to go when the time comes. Wonder if she was like this when she came, or whether it's working with whackos that does it? Obediently he followed her and changed into a hospital gown, wondering why hospital clothing had to leave the whole backside exposed and why everything about hospitals seemed to be designed to take away the patient's self respect. The Lady Sonia showed him how to climb into a sort of network hammock slung between the two ends of a sunken bath.

"You're going to love this," she gushed. "While you're here I want you to think of nothing else but FLOATING ON THE SURFACE OF THE WATER LIKE A WATER LILY." Once again she caroled, and once again her right hand sailed the air.

"But why can't I just lie in the bath?" he asked. "Why do I have to be strapped in this strait-jacket like a suet pudding?"

"That's to force you to relax, dear," she explained. "No movement, no pressure, no thoughts. Just a water lily."

As the water rose beneath him Lawton felt not so much like a water lily as a ship in dry-dock. The hammock was fairly comfortable, but he had never been able to lie still without moving his limbs, and the restriction was irksome. As the water swirled gently round him he had to admit it was a pleasant enough sensation. But if he were designing it he would have used a soft airbed instead of the hammock, and allowed arms and legs to float free. And a pillow for his head.

It was at that moment that the gurgling water, not content with merely swirling round him, began to swirl the bath as well. Faster and faster the bath revolved till the walls of the room became a blur. Then the voice came clearly to him above the noise of the rushing water.

"You have forty eight hours to file a written report of the accident, Sir."

The first thing he saw was the uniform. Then the man inside the uniform, and the police car. And the car in front of his, the one with the buckled trunk. The police officer signed the ticket and tore it off the pad. "You can take the report in at the same time you pay the fine. This lady will want your name and address and license number and details of your insurance."

A typical Chesney situation thought Lawton. If he'd smelled my breath! Or seen the bulge in my pocket! This could have got me a DWI and a concealed weapon and a firearms license rap all in one package. Bad enough to have to suffer the Changes without the kind of troubles Chesney can get me into. Got to stop carrying this gun about with me. He took the citation and his license from the officer and turned to face the owner of the other car, a memory of water lilies in the bathtub vaguely in his mind.

But if I leave the gun in the apartment that meathead may get hold of it and ditch it. Better that than have something like this happen again, though. Getting another gun's as easy as buying a hamburger, and whatever it costs it's going to be worth it to get rid of all this Wainright crap.

* * *

Meanwhile, back at the hospital, Charlie Chesney was not prepared to find himself apparently about to drown. His first reaction was to scream.

"Help!" he screamed in instant panic. "I'm drowning! For god's sake get me out of here!" But almost at once, as memory and awareness took his brain in tow, the more urgent fear was for the comfort of his ears.

"I can't take water in my ears," he screamed. "I've got holes in my eardrums. I've got to keep my ears out of water. Turn this bloody thing off! Nurse! Is anyone out there? For Crissake pull your finger out of your ass and do something! Nur—se!"

But no one heard. No one was within earshot. Doctor Wainright had been ordered to relax for thirty minutes. Charlie kept his ears above the water level by raising his head as far as he could, but without the leverage of his arms it was an intolerable strain on the muscles of his neck. Swearing with all the picturesqueness he had first learned in the circus, he struggled to break the straps that held the net closed about him. But his arms were straight down by his sides. All his struggling achieved was to tilt him sideways, and threaten to tip him face down into the water. The more he struggled, the more the water invaded his ears. No real damage would result, but he was beyond reason, fighting the water, fighting the restraining net, fighting his very presence in the bath.

Screaming, shouting, crying, cursing, he strained and writhed. Without being consciously aware of any new technique, he found there was enough slack to let him draw up his knees slightly, and then kick out again with his feet. It was the only movement he could make. Kick by vicious kick the ring on the end strap weakened till at last it parted, dumping his legs to the bottom. He was fortunate it was the ring at his feet that broke, and not the one at his head, or he would have drowned. It was another five minutes before his manic strength broke open one side of the net. With savage fury he tore the mesh apart. The hospital gown wrapped itself soppingly about him as he staggered out onto the floor, one sleeve ripped off in the struggle and all four tapes parted at the back. With a howl of rage he ripped it from his body and flung himself naked at the door, hell-bent on a rampage of destruction.

But the door was locked. After a fusillade of kicks had threatened to break his naked toes he gave up attacking it and stood leaning with his head against the wall, sobbing and cursing, mentally and physically exhausted. When the Nurse Supervisor eventually found him he was curled up on the floor asleep, the demolished net, the discarded gown and the flooded floor a testament to his mindless frenzy.

They gave him a sedative, took him to a very small, barely furnished room, and put him gently to bed. His body was scored with livid weals caused by the struggle inside the net. Four toes were bleeding from raw places where the skin had been abraded by his attack on the door. The Water Lily Treatment would not go down in history as one of Alex Wronski's better ideas.

The room was barely furnished because it had been designed to house a patient with a tendency to hurt himself. The bed was bolted to the floor. A metal wardrobe was screwed into the wall. There was room for little else. The window was made of armored glass. A small sliding panel set at eye-level in the door allowed the patient to be observed from the corridor outside. And of course the door was locked.

Throughout the evening, the observation hatch was slid aside at regular intervals, but the patient who had been admitted in the name of Lawton Wainright slept on well into the night. When at last he awoke, the fear and rage had all drained out of him. Lethargy had overtaken his sedated brain, and he was content to lie quietly dozing and let the images of the past few days drift haphazardly past in review.

Three times the little shutter in the door opened and closed, and gradually the bits and bytes in Charlie Chesney's mind became ordered enough to form themselves into a pattern of lucid thought. It was his act that was uppermost in his mind. But then the museum began to intrude. The Board had been most gracious when he broke the news that he had to go to hospital for a few days. The confrontation with Miss Gwynn had not after all materialized—Miss Gwynn had sent word she was too indisposed to attend the meeting. So there had been considerable satisfaction in knowing he had not run away from the issue, and that he after all had more moral strength than Old Ironsides herself.

As he drifted in and out of sleep the lucid thoughts broke into garbled fragments, and then formed back into coherent patterns again. Sometimes he felt like Lawton Wainright. Sometimes Charlie Chesney took over. And all the while the little sliding hatch that looked across at him marked the passage of the hours. He could tell when it was opened without looking, by the sound it made. At first he looked up each time, expecting to be able to see the observing eyeball peering through. But the door was in shadow. It was difficult to tell whether the shutter was open or closed other than by the sound. What were they looking for, he wondered. To see if he was awake? To make sure he was still there? What would they do if he wasn't there? Eventually he could think of nothing else. All there was in life was the waiting, then the rattle and slide, the pause, another rattle and slide, and then silence while he waited till the time came round again. If only he could see the face! Or even the eye. Perhaps it wasn't a face? Perhaps it was a robot with a camera? Or a microscope? He was the specimen under the microscope and they were trying to find out if he was taking care of Wainright's body while he occupied it.

There had to be some way he could get out from under that microscope. Somewhere they wouldn't be able to see him. The cupboard? Stealthily he climbed out of bed and tried the cupboard door. Locked. Goddam! Did they lock everything around here? He'd throw something at the stupid face next time it peered in. But there was nothing to throw, only a pillow, and there was no satisfaction in that.

It was a young lady with the unlikely name of Monica Upfelt who made the discovery. Unlikely only because she most certainly had not been, not for several weeks, and she was missing it.

Casually opening the hatch of Room 27 just as she had several times before that night, she saw that the bed was unoccupied. Applying her eye more closely to the aperture, she inspected all areas of the room. The patient was nowhere to be seen. She looked across at the window, which certainly appeared inviolate. Anyway it was made of armored glass.

She ran agitatedly back to the Nurses' Room, where the Shift Nurse was talking on the phone. "He's gone!" she announced breathlessly.

"Room twenty seven, he's not there."

"He must be." The Shift Nurse was not to be panicked. Her name tag said 'Patience.'

"I can't see him. Had we better go in?"

"We're not supposed to. He might be violent."

"Well we've got to do something. He might be loose in the hospital."

"Did you check if the door was locked?"

"No," Miss Upfelt admitted. "I ran straight back here."

Patience sighed. "I'll have to hang up," she told the telephone. "It's going to be one of those nights."

Together they went back to Room 27. Patience peered through the panel, inspecting this way and that. She quietly turned the door handle and pushed. "It's still locked," she announced. "Shoot! Why does this have to happen on my shift?"

"Mine too," said Miss Upfelt with feeling.

Back in the Nurses' Room Patience telephoned the Shift Nurse of the Medical Wing. "Stella, one of my patients is missing. What the hell do I do?"

"How about resigning?" suggested Stella.

"Is that the best you can do? Do you think I should call Wronski at home?"

"Don't ask me dear. Not my department. Have you searched?"

"No. His door's still locked."

"Then he must be still in there," decided the practical Stella. "Search the room."

"We're not supposed to go in without approval."

"For god's sake, what if he's having a heart attack? Do you have to get approval then?"

"I guess not. But he was under sedation. He might be violent."

"Jim's up here. I'll send him down."

With the night boiler man in support, they returned to Room 27 and unlocked the door, entering cautiously. There was no occupant.

"The cupboard," said the boiler man, taking charge. But the cupboard was locked.

"Under the bed," said the boiler man. But the bed was enclosed on all sides right down to the floor.

"He didn't get out of the window," Miss Upfelt said, "so . . ."

"So someone must have let him out," pronounced the boiler man. "He must be on the loose. Is he a loony?"

"Don't let Professor Wronski hear you say that," said Patience severely, "or you'll be looking for another boiler. His file just says he's in for observation. I think I'd better alert the other departments, and you'd better see if he's anywhere about here. Monica, you and Jim check every room on this floor. Check the beds, the cupboards, everywhere."

By the time Alex Wronski had dressed and driven from his residence, there was uproar throughout the hospital. Sleeping patients, whether medical or surgical, were wakened and their beds searched in case the missing man should have jumped into bed with one of them. Wronski himself had called in the Police, more with an eye to the appearance of the evidence he might have to give at any future enquiry than with a city-wide manhunt in mind. Doctor Wainright had not been certified, after all. He was not even legally a patient. He had the right to leave whenever he liked. But leaving without unlocking the door was being inconsiderate.

He made first for the Nurses' Room and gathered up Patience and Miss Upfelt. The gentleman known as Jim was still there, finding the occasion a welcome change from sitting waiting for a boiler to burst. His assistant had also arrived from some limbo of pipe wrenches and dirty coffee cups, together with two City policemen with guns.

It was therefore a confident group of six who followed Wronski to Room 27. The door had locked itself again after Lawton's absence had been discovered. And it was some minutes before Patience could remember where she had put the key for safety. With the door unlocked, Professor Wronski stepped warily inside the little room and stopped, looking around for any sign of his patient. Six would-be spectators of various sizes and momentum pressed into the doorway after him. The tide poured through the door until, two nurses, two policemen, one boiler man and one apprentice later, the door swung closed and they stood like commuters in a Tokyo subway train.

"Just as well he isn't here," remarked one of the policeman. "There wouldn't be room for him anyway. Let's get out of here."

"Yes, everybody out of here!" shouted Professor Wronski with considerable acerbity. "This isn't a side-show at a circus. Open the door."

But the door had locked itself. More Patience than Prudence, the Shift Nurse had left the key in the lock outside the door. Seven voices raised their clamor all at once. Several fists began to pound upon the door.

And then, above the din, a voice was heard loudly to complain, "Jeeesus Christ! Is there no way I can get some sleep in this madhouse? You sound like a bunch of nuns at a jock-strap sale!"

The clamor ceased abruptly. Six faces looked as if their owners had heard a message from the dead. Professor Wronski alone had the wit to look up to where the voice had seemed to be. Above their heads, extended comfortably along the top of the grey steel wardrobe, lay the naked figure of Lawton Wainright.

CHAPTER 19

Charles Delano Chesney, Junior, was not used to waking up to an empty bed. Quite often, waking with a pounding head and a furry mouth, he had not known what kind of companion to expect beside him. It would be feminine, he could be sure of that, but whether white or black, blonde or brunette, depended on where he had been the night before. And in the first few hazy minutes of a Morning After, he could not always be sure about that. But during the past few days, his main concern on waking had been less about who was in his bed than whose bed he was in. Like Lawton Wainright, the quality of his day depended to a great extent on whether he woke in the bedroom at Park Plaza or the boudoir at Croftdown Road. Even though The Changes seemed to be happening at more unpredictable times, there was always the chance he could have changed while he slept, as had happened on the first few occasions.

That first waking moment had become an important moment in the day. If The Change had happened overnight, there was a slightly better chance he could get through the day without suffering the trauma of finding himself attacked by a female ape or drowning in a lily pond. And once again it had happened overnight, and he was back in his own apartment again.

The previous day had started in the hospital. They had let him out of the little cubicle with the shutter in the door (getting themselves out had occupied most of the night, he recalled with satisfaction), and they certainly wouldn't be trying that damn fool Water Lily treatment again. But damn Wainright anyway! There never would have been any Water Lily treatment if Wainright hadn't gone to ground at the University like a rabbit in a rainstorm.

Everything Wainright touched he loused up. It was bad enough having to suffer the Changes, but why of all people did he have to get stuck with a longhaired droop like Wainright?

But that was all in the past, he told himself grimly. He was himself again. So today was The Day. After today there would be no more Changes. No more Wainright. No more having his life loused up for him. He couldn't go on any longer. And he certainly didn't intend going on taking Wainright's place in the booby hatch. With a nurse who was a certifiable whacko! Wainright might be able to take it, but not Cheerful Charlie Chesney.

The phone interrupted his thoughts. It was Linda. "Charlie," she said, "I'm worried about you."

"Save it!" he told her. "I can take care of myself."

"Charlie! Don't be so bitter. I wanted to stay and help you through all this awfulness. You must be terribly lonely all by yourself?"

"Drop the other shoe," he said. "You didn't call just to pat my head."

"I feel guilty about helping Lawton and leaving you. I want to be able to help you too. Charlie, why don't you go out to the University and work with Alex? If he had you and Lawton together he could watch the two of you change. And if you were both out there you'd know what you were getting into each time. Alex says now he's seen you after you've changed with Lawton he wants to see you as you really are."

"You're off your trolley, Baby," Charlie sneered. "I've been out there, remember? I've seen it. It's a mad- house. I'd have to be nuts to go out there."

"Think about it, Charlie. Alex says he thinks he could find the way out more quickly if you'd work with him."

"Tell Alex to blow it out his ass. You too Baby." He hung up.

No way was he going to get involved with Wronski. There was only one way out, and that was to get rid of Wainright. He'd have to get another gun—the clown had ditched the gun during The Change the day before. Did he think it was the only gun in the world? That's what pawnshops were for. And gun laws. To make it easy. The plan was clear in his mind. The only way it could possibly go wrong was if they had a Change before he could get to Wainright. In which case he'd just have to wait for another day. But they had just changed overnight, after midnight actually, because he had stayed up watching television in his room till nearly one-thirty. So past experience indicated he should have most of the day clear at least. Wainright would be going out for his exercise stint between two and four. That was when he'd be accessible. Alone. So the deed would be done by four.

The University was in nearly five hundred acres of land gifted half a century before under an endowment plan by an oil baron. Some of the land outside the University proper had been used for faculty residences. But most was still unspoiled woodland, a green belt guaranteeing protection from the suburban sprawl that had already, amoebae-like, surrounded it and threatened to engulf it. The hospital area was on the periphery of the campus, looking out over Five Elm Wood and down the slope to where the lake lay hidden in the trees. Under the terms of the endowment, the land was to be made accessible to the public at all times, yet few people took advantage of the rural haven within the confines of the city limits. It was a rustic shelter in a secluded part of the bird sanctuary that Professor Wronski had suggested Lawton should use for relaxation.

"Take a book down there and enjoy the peace and quiet and fresh air," he said. "You can relax there, and we shall know where you are if we want you."

Chesney would probably have walked the other way on principle rather than comply, but Wainright would do as he was told. He'd pee his pants if Wronski said so, Chesney told himself derisively.

At eleven o'clock, Charlie Chesney left the apartment and drove downtown to a pawnshop on East Main where the proprietor bought and sold a variety of merchandise with the minimum of paper work. He walked through to the rear of the shop, to a windowless storeroom uncluttered by the cameras and binoculars and stereos and wristwatches that filled the front of the store. From an impressive array of toys for terrorists, he selected a small automatic that would fit easily into his inside jacket pocket without showing a bulge. God bless the gun crazies for making this possible, he thought. He drove to the Prince of Wales, a pseudo-English pub whose owner had been an actor in his younger days. He drank three gin and tonics in the space of an hour, and ordered lunch with the last one.

Earlier in the morning, when Linda had called, his determination to get rid of Wainright had been an obsession, one that excited him and brought his heart beat up into his throat. Now all that had passed. His heart was beating normally. His brain was calm and clear. He knew exactly what he had to do. The schedule he had planned allowed him to do the ordinary things that filled an ordinary day. As he ate his lunch, he might have been preparing for an afternoon at the track, he noted with approval. He thought about his accountant's suggestion that he buy a restaurant. Or a pub. Good publicity. As well as bringing in the dough. He thought about the convertible in the parking lot, and wondered whether he should turn it for a new one.

At one fifteen, after a leisurely lunch, he drove to the Public Safety building to pay his traffic fine and submit the written report of the accident. It pleased his sense of the dramatic to walk into the very heart of the city police force with a murder plan in his mind and the weapon in his pocket. Soon after one forty five he was leaving Sears parking lot with a pair of binoculars, a copy of the Audubon Field Guide To North American Birds and a pair of thin gloves. He drove just below the speed limit. No point in having his schedule spoiled by being stopped for a traffic offense, and he had no intention of arriving before Wainright was in position, or of wasting time looking at more birds than was absolutely necessary.

The main driveway from the Seventh Avenue bus loop to the campus proper was a wide, grass-lined boulevard that wound for nearly a mile between the woods on either side. Close to the loop the boulevard was divided by a center median. The entrance to the boulevard was flanked by lichen covered stonework gateposts, relics of the days of the old private estate. Inside the entrance, tastefully constructed of matching stone, a small security post commanded the road. Charlie Chesney stopped at the security post, and smiled benignly over half-moon glasses at the red-blazered young lady in the kiosk.

"Good afternoon to you," he said in a slightly European accent. "I'm going to spend some time in the Reference Library. Do I need a pass?"

"Just a parking permit, Sir. Will you sign the visitors' book, please?"

He signed 'Marschal Korder' in the book. "Just leave the permit on the dash," the young lady told him. "Do you know your way? Then here's a map of the campus. You are here. This is the Reference Library. Visitor parking is marked in green. You can use any one of the visitor parking lots, but this is the one nearest to the library." She marked a cross in red pencil on one of the green shaded areas. "The Reference Library building is number seven."

"Thank you, young lady," Chesney said. "You've been most helpful."

"Have a nice day," she recited.

No point in advertising that I'm going to the bird sanctuary, he thought as he drove off, maintaining a sedate pace up the boulevard.

His eye was caught by flashing lights in his rear mirror. A police car was overtaking him. Now what the hell is this all about? Instinctively he checked his speedometer, slowing down without obviously braking. The patrol car slowed behind him, gave a perfunctory wail on the siren. For the first time, the detached calm that had been with him throughout the day began to crack and he felt his heart thumping with apprehension. He stopped. The patrol car stopped behind him. The officer walked forward toward him, taking his time. As he came to the window, Chesney saw the words on his shoulder, 'University Police.' Same difference, he thought. It could be the Girl Scouts. I just don't need trouble right now.

"You Marshal Corder?" asked the officer, leaning on the door.

"Yes officer, that's me," Chesney said, smiling. He was too close to the security kiosk to deny it. And no other car had driven in since.

"You just drive in, Sir?"

"Yes," he said.

"Security want to see you. Will you drive back to the entrance, please."

They couldn't have anything on him. No one knew he was coming. They couldn't even know who he was. Unless the girl had recognized him in spite of the glasses.

"You can make a U-turn here," the officer said. "Stop on the other side of the road inside the entrance, please."

Chesney made the U-turn, and drove back on the other side of the median. The police car turned and followed him. Unobtrusively he felt his jacket pocket, checking whether the bulge showed. She couldn't have noticed that. He parked just inside the entrance. The police car stopped behind him. Halfway across the road he remembered the half-moon glasses. His disguise! He had taken them off for driving. He looked back. The police car was still there. He decided to brazen it out.

The lady in red was talking on the phone. She looked across at him. "Mister Korder?"

"Yes?" he said.

"Lucky the patrol was down this end, or I wouldn't have caught you. You left your parking permit in the visitors' register. Might have had your car towed away without it."

For once Charlie Chesney was speechless. Relief was superceded by indignation. Stupid broad! Damn nearly made a run for it. Could have ruined the whole thing. Why couldn't she tell the goddam cop it was nothing serious? He took the pass from her mechanically, belatedly remembering his pose of geniality, and thanked her with the best grace he could muster. The mood was spoiled! All day he had felt like a professional killer, cold, emotionless, confident, ruthless. Now he was once again an ordinary man committed to a far from ordinary deed. The plan had been infallible before. Now he realized it only needed a bomb scare in the parking lot, a flat tire, a thunderstorm, and he was up the creek. What was it they said about a butterfly in Peking changing the whole course of events? Perhaps the silly bitch had done him a favor after all? Brought him down to earth. Pricked the bubble of unfounded optimism that had been surrounding him. Made him more careful.

As he drove up the boulevard, he picked out from the map one of the visitors' parking lots that would give him access to Five Elm Wood. He had no wish to be seen near the hospital, in case anything should go wrong. He was a little later than he had planned, but he still had forty minutes before Wainright would be returning to the hospital. He parked the car, and almost immediately found a rustic sign pointing the way to the bird sanctuary. He had his binoculars slung round his neck and the Field Guide in his hand for the sake of appearance. The walking trails were well trodden, but by the time he reached the lake he had still met no one on the trail. Of course, there was no guarantee that Wainright would be in the shelter. He might be anywhere on the trail round the lake. He wondered whether his subconscious was even now talking to Wainright, persuading him to sit in the shelter as Wronski had suggested. Strange to think he might be talking to him, yet he had no way of knowing.

One thing he knew. Killing a man was not the cold, dispassionate act it had seemed when he was planning it. He was nervous. Frightened. What if he should bungle it? Only injure Wainright without killing him? He didn't really want to hurt him. Only get rid of him. He had to. One of them had to go, and he certainly wasn't going to kill himself.

He put on the gloves and took the gun out of his pocket. He had already polished it clean of fingerprints.

It was dangerous to put off the safety-catch now, but he dare not risk forgetting it at the crucial moment. The feel of the gun in his hand made him feel better. Only a short while, and it would all be over. Put the gun in Wainright's dead hand, and high tail it back to the car. There was no one about. Besides, people didn't usually come running if they heard a shot. They stayed out of the way. Or else they assumed it was somebody hunting. Or hoped it was.

Before he was expecting it, he came upon the shelter, thirty feet away down the trail. The open side was away from him, so it was impossible to tell whether Wainright was there. What if there was someone with him? That was a possibility he had forgotten in his planning. He put his right hand with the gun into the side pocket of his jacket, fumbling awkwardly with gloved hands. Then, quietly, he approached the shelter and looked inside. Wainright was there, alone.

CHAPTER 20

It might have been a sound or a flickering shadow, but something made Lawton Wainright look up from his book. A man was watching from the shadows outside the shelter. Chesney! He recognized the face immediately, a face he had grown to know so well, though he had only seen it once before. Other than in the mirror. His heart began to pump wildly. Chesney could only be there for one purpose. He had thought he was so secure in the heart of the University grounds, but Chesney had tracked him down.

He was all alone, and Chesney had a gun. There might be someone else walking through the woods, someone he could call to. He could feel the panic rising, but this time it was more under control. It was the fear of being stalked like an animal that had so terrified him before. This time the danger was present, visible, immediate, and he had to face it.

He watched Chesney put his right hand in his pocket. He could make a run for it and hope Chesney would miss. He could try to wrestle the gun away, but he had never done anything physical like that, and he had no idea how to go about it. Or even whether he could get to him in time. And then the gun was out of Chesney's pocket and pointing at him and it was too late to take any action anyway. The only hope was that someone might come along the path. If only he could keep Chesney talking. Or even talk him out of using the gun. Try to sound calm. Persuade Chesney it would be as bad living with a conscience as living with The Changes. What would Linda suggest? She wouldn't want him to act like a wimp.

"A pity we have to have a gun between us the first time we actually meet face to face," he said, trying to sound calm. What would James Bond do? There must be some way of turning the tables.

"Pity we ever met in the first place," Chesney said. "Pity for you, anyway. This is bye-bye, Wainright. I don't feel like hanging about talking."

"You're nervous," Lawton taunted him. Keep talking. Someone might come. "You're not so tough as you pretend. I don't think you've ever fired that thing before."

Suddenly the seat beneath him began to tip sideways.

He had to put his hand down for support. The whole shelter was swaying, and then beginning to spin, and the dizziness began to overtake him and it was the sensation he had felt so many times before. In the distance he heard a voice, Chesney's voice, shouting out. "God no! Not now! Not yet for crissake!"

When the motion ceased, and Lawton was able to open his eyes again, he was standing outside the shelter. The other man was sitting on the seat where he had been. The other man? It was his own face looking at him. His own clothes. It was himself. As he had said, this was the first time they had actually met face to face, but this was the wrong face with the wrong man. And the wrong man had the gun in his hand. He looked down at it, wondering what he should do. He had never fired a gun before, and anyway he had no mind to kill. Besides, the man on the seat was himself. He would be killing himself. A conversation with Wronski was vaguely in the back of his mind, something Wronski had said that must be important, but he was too confused to recall it.

Chesney was evidently terrified by the turn of events, shrinking back white faced into the far corner of the shelter. Slowly he raised his hand, slowly so as not to alarm Wainright. "Put it away," he pleaded. "The safety catch is off. It could go off, and you're not used to guns."

Lawton was beginning to feel more secure. "There doesn't seem to be much to it," he said, pointing the gun experimentally. "You just point it and shoot, don't you? I've seen it on television. Only you do it close up so as to get powder burns and make it look like suicide. Isn't that the way you wanted to do it?" He moved a step closer and aimed at Chesney.

Charlie Chesney began to shake. "You wouldn't do it. You wouldn't kill me. You can't. I wasn't really going to kill you. I meant to, but I swear at the last minute I wouldn't have been able to do it. Don't kill me. I'll come and work with Wronski. I'll do anything you say."

Lawton was gaining more confidence with the gun. He had found the safety catch, and flipped it on and off a few times till Chesney lost count of whether it was on or off.

"Feels different at the other end of the manhunt, doesn't it? I told you the other day you hadn't got much going for you. It looks as if I was right. There's not much manhood in you, is there?"

Chesney was trembling so hard the book on his lap slipped to the ground. "Please!" he whispered. "Don't do it."

"Don't worry," Lawton said. "I'm not going to. But it was an interesting experience while it lasted. Gives you quite a feeling of power, doesn't it?"

Chesney relaxed and a little color returned to his face. "Listen to me," he pleaded urgently. "Put the safety catch on and listen. There's no need to have a shoot out. We can sort this out in Wronski's office." He held out his hand. "Give me the gun. It could go off if you play with it like that."

Lawton laughed. "You do think I'm naive, don't you?

I think the best place for this thing is in the lake. I certainly don't trust you with it."

He turned away. Chesney leaped up from the seat and lunged for Lawton's right arm in one frantic movement. The gun slipped from Lawton's hand and fell to the ground between them. Chesney elbowed him violently in the stomach and stooped quickly to pick up the gun.

"You bloody fool," he snarled. "If you want to go slowly mad I don't. I came here to put an end to this and there's no way you're going to stop me." He put the gun to Lawton's head, staring into his eyes.

Slowly an appalled expression came over his face. "Jeeeezus!" he exclaimed lowering the gun. "I must be crazy already. That's my face!

That's my head! I'm just about to blow my own brains out! You'd like that, wouldn't you? That's what you wanted, you clever bastard. Let me kill myself so you can have it all your own way."

He backed away from Lawton, back to the seat he had left. Lawton was still struggling for breath. "You don't understand," he gasped. "I've been talking to Wronski. We really have changed places. Wronski says . . ."

"Wronski can blow it! That's my body and I want it back in one piece. You had me worried just now when you pointed that thing over here. But this is your body. I should have let you shoot it. You're the one who's making the big exit, Wainright."

He sat back down, picked up the book Lawton had been reading and put the gun to his head. "I planned it to look like suicide, and this way it's sure as hell going to be suicide. Wainright's head with a hole in it, and Wainright's finger on the trigger."

"Don't do it," Lawton shouted urgently. "That's my body, and you may blow it's brains out. But it's Chesney inside right now. You'll be killing yourself."

"Not bloody likely I won't. Don't try to bullshit me, Wainright. Chesney doesn't belong in this scrawny little frame, and Chesney's not staying. Bye-bye, Wainright."

He pulled the trigger.

Lawton Wainright had never before been close to a gun when it was fired. The noise was numbing to every sense. A high-pitched whistle in his ears blanked out all sound and conscious thought. He stood paralyzed, and even though his eyes watched the body slump sideways on the seat, the movement hardly registered in his mind. It was several seconds before he began to think again. The shattered skull and the blood already spreading across the seat should have sickened him. He had never in his life been close to any sort of violence. And yet his first sensation was one of blank surprise that he could look so calmly and objectively at his own body lying mutilated on the seat. His body. But who had died inside that shell? Not Lawton Wainright, certainly. Poor Chesney! He must have been quite unbalanced at the end. And after all he had miscalculated. He thought he could escape the dead shell of Lawton's body. But instead he had died with it.

He looked down at the body he was occupying, Chesney's body encased in Chesney's clothes. Tasteless, inelegant clothes. And felt disgust. He had worn them during The Changes in the past, but now they seemed alien, out of place. He tried to think why Chesney should have wanted to wear such things, and found no thoughts of Chesney's in his mind. He could remember where Chesney lived, because he had been there during those terrible Changes. But all the memories of Chesney's life, his childhood, his career, his problems and successes, were gone. Chesney was gone. With one of them gone there could be no more Changes, Chesney had said. Well, one of them was gone.

He remembered so clearly the terror of that first morning when his reflection had looked out at him with Chesney's face. Yet now he was facing reasonably calmly the fact that his reflection would always look out at him with Chesney's face. Chesney's bleary eyes and puffy face were his, he had inherited them. As he seemed to have inherited everything else of Chesneys.

He was still wearing the gloves Chesney must have put on specially for the occasion. So the only fingerprints on the gun would be Lawton's. It had been meant to look like suicide, and it certainly had been suicide. The gun was still gripped in the right hand. His right hand, the hand he had used so often and would never use again. Poor Alex Wronski! He had tried to help, and now they would bring him Wainright's body and say he shot himself, and Alex would blame himself and agonize because he had lost a patient. Even though he wasn't officially a patient. But Lawton had lost more than that. Lawton had lost a body. He felt his eyes becoming blurred by tears, but felt no shame. Surely he could weep for his own passing? Claire certainly wouldn't.

It occurred to him that this was no time to stay and mourn. He needed to get away before anyone came. Chesney's car would be in the nearest parking lot, he guessed. He felt no twinge of conscience at leaving the scene. This was Chesney's crime, not his.

He walked quickly up the trail, wondering where he should go. Not to the hospital, not even to collect his things. They were no longer his things. Lawton Wainright was dead. Not home to Croftdown Road. That had been Lawton Wainright's home, and Wainright was dead. Besides, he didn't even have the key to the house any more. He gave the car its head like a horse out on the trail, and let it drive him while his mind attempted to adjust to all that being dead implied. Who was he? Was he a non-person now, a man with no identity?

He was climbing out of the car at the Park Plaza apartments before he realized where he was. Chesney's apartment. As good a place as anywhere. He had the key. And he could phone Linda and tell her everything that had happened. The main door of the complex was equipped with the latest thing in security, an electronic device that read the handprint and matched it with those stored in its memory. He presented his hand.

"Thank you Mister Chesney," the computer said with digital satisfaction at knowing it was right, and released the lock. At least the computer was sure who he was.

He took the elevator. By the time he had let himself into the apartment, he knew what he should do. Counseling by computer, he thought. Let a piece of software make the important decisions in your life. The computer said he was Mr. Chesney, so presumably he was Charlie Chesney. He dialed Linda's office number, hoping she would still be there. There was no answer, not even a secretary. He dialed her apartment, wondering if she would be home yet.

"Linda darling," he said when he heard her voice. "I've got a lot to tell you about. The main thing is, it's all over. Yes, it's all finished. No, it wasn't because of Wronski. Yes, I'll tell you all about it when I see you. But there's something more important right now.

"Do you think you could stand being Mrs. Lawton Chesney for the rest of your life?"

The End

SYNOPSIS

This is a sometimes-humorous look at a traumatic psychological entanglement.

Of the three main characters, Lawton Wainright, a decent but stuffy archaeologist trapped in an unhappy marriage, is the character with whom the reader empathizes. He is the respected Director of the Museum of Anthropology.

Cheerful Charlie Chesney, the star turn at the Tight Owl nightclub, is his antithesis—brash, amoral and hard drinking.

Linda McClusky is caught up in the plot when she takes Charlie home to sober him up and becomes his latest girl.

When Lawton wakes one morning to find himself in a strange bed, in a strange apartment, with a strange girl, and inhabiting Charlie Chesney's body, the predicament brings stark terror. It is only the warmth and sympathy of Linda that carries him through the day.

Charlie, meanwhile, has been faced with the even worse situation of finding himself in Lawton's body and coping with Lawton's bitchy wife.

When Lawton wakes up the following day to find himself safely back in his own bed and his own body, his relief is tempered by a longing for Linda. And when the trauma he calls The Change happens again, Linda is there to ameliorate the terror.

The Changes become more frequent, and each finds himself passing for the other and doing the other's job, though retaining his own basic character. But The Changes become more unpredictable, and each finds himself unexpectedly plunged into embarrassing situations generated by the other. Lawton, inhabited by Charlie, seduces his eager secretary and his frigid boss, jeopardizes his job and loses his wife. Charlie antagonizes his audience and loses his nightclub contract.

Linda, Charlie's girl, finds herself falling in love with the personality of Lawton when he occupies Charlie's body, though feeling disloyal to Charlie. Lawton finds himself equally in love with Linda and looking forward to The Changes in order to be with her.

The strain on each of the three mounts as each reacts in a different way. Linda finds it impossible to live with a man with two personalities, never knowing which of the two she will wake up to in the morning. Lawton feels suicidal. Charlie reasons that, with one of them out of the way The Changes must cease, and so encourages Lawton's suicide.

After various ridiculous incidents in a T/V studio, a psychiatrist's office and a research establishment, during which The Change inevitably happens at an inopportune moment, Charlie sets out to end the problem by shooting Lawton.

As he confronts Lawton with gun in hand, the final act takes place. The problem is solved!!!

475-ALLE

175-ALLE

90000>
9 780738 832937